ANOTHER MAN'S SHOES

D.C. PAGE

PAGE PUBLISHING, INC.
Conneaut Lake, PA

First originally published by Page Publishing 2022

ISBN 978-1-6624-4869-0 (pbk)
ISBN 978-1-6624-5245-1 (hc)
ISBN 978-1-6624-4870-6 (digital)

Printed in the United States of America

To my wife, Terry Page,
who has always supported my creative efforts
and given me the love, family, and
opportunity to pursue my dreams

ACKNOWLEDGMENTS

My parents, Cleora and Charles Page
Gordon D. Sykes
S. C. Sykes
Mary Mooney

I want to thank all the members of the health-
care community for every act of kindness they so
willingly share with those who are disabled.

Special thanks to Joshua Cooper Page, Matthew David
Page, Michael Austin Page, and Jason Charles Page

NEW SHOES

Gordon walked me through his house, garage, and yard. Well, I walked. He rolled. He had been in a wheelchair for decades. We were discussing the details of his will, following a three-hour appointment with his lawyer.

"The access vans, wheelchairs, hospital bed, and other medical equipment are to be donated to the Veterans Association," Gordon said, calmly, without emotion. "The furniture, bedclothes, towels, and kitchen things can be given to the Salvation Army."

I took notes as we went from space to space but more to appear as if I was paying attention than anything else. Gordon had been dying for forty years, and I just didn't think his death was any closer than it had ever been. Death had been part of the threesome since the beginning. Like a silent partner, he was always in the room but had never taken an unbeatable stand on any particular issue. Yes, there were bouts of pneumonia, infections, and bedsores along with constant bladder problems, but despite all predictions, they were hampered by antibiotics and sheer will power. Little did I know that each time death was beaten back into submission, he never stopped contemplating a complete takeover.

"The prints and paintings I've collected over the years, along with the little knickknacks are yours, if you want them. There are about five thousand books in the house. I've read them all at least twice. Take what interests you. Donate the rest to the library. My pencil drawings are what I'm most concerned about. Would you take them? Being a quadriplegic, there's not much else I can point at and say, 'I did that.' What do you think?"

"I'll treasure them, Gordon."

"Good! Now that's settled. Don't let anyone else tell you that I promised them one of these, 'cause I didn't. I want them to be yours."

We were quiet for a moment as we looked around at the impossible. Numerous large, framed, exquisitely detailed portraits hung everywhere, and Gordon had done each one. Using one of his twisted hands and his mouth, he had convinced a pencil into doing his bidding. He based his drawings on photographs of famous people that would never know him. He chose faces that were beautiful or different or challenging to tame by a piece of lead. He would start by making a grid, isolating a few inches at a time on which to concentrate his efforts. Over many weeks, one filled grid merged with another and then another until a face appeared on the drawing board. Each face took time, a lot of time, sometimes years!

"Of course, I'll take them!" I reassured. "I've always loved them."

"Good! Now let's look in the closet."

Dutifully, I followed the whir of his electric chair down the hall and around the corner. "If any of these shirts or sweaters fit, take them home and give the rest to Goodwill. Check out the new shoes in that box. I think they're your size. I liked the style and foolishly bought two pairs years ago. Shoes don't wear out when you're stuck in a chair! You walk in them! Give them a good workout! I like the thought of you walking in my shoes. You've always taken me with words to where I've been unable to go."

"Anything else for the list?" I asked a little too impatiently. I wanted to get on with life and put all this death talk on hold.

"Yes! The house! I'm afraid I'm leaving you a mess, David. There is a lot to do here. The place needs a new roof, and there are multiple other repairs that must be done before you can even put it on the market. There won't be much money left. There are many bills to be paid." He stopped abruptly, rotating in his chair, and looked up at me, startled, as if he just realized for the first time all he was asking me to do. "Are you sure you want to take this on? It's all going to require work and keep you in California for a long time. Your home and family are in Pennsylvania. It won't be easy."

"We're brothers, aren't we?" I interrupted. "No problem. Don't worry. Are we through now? I thought we were going out for Mexican tonight and a couple of margaritas!"

I got him into the van and then out again at our favorite Mexican restaurant, not fully realizing all that I had agreed to.

I held the taco to his mouth for each bite and got him a straw for his margarita, adjusting the glass so he could lean into the edge of the table for each sip. I'd wipe his face with a napkin and periodically take him to empty his urine bag. We talked, made obscene comments, and laughed, making believe I'd never really need that list. We pretended, like we pretended we were brothers. We weren't. Neither of us had a brother, so we chose each other. He also chose me to be his power of attorney, and I chose to accept. There really wasn't any choice at all.

"One thing more," he blurted out between gulps. "I have a particular account that I want you to take care of. There is a woman who was my special nurse when I first went to the hospital, following the accident. You'll find her address in the little black book next to the phone. I want you to get a certified check for fifty thousand dollars and send it to her. Sony left me a little money when she died. Use those funds. You may be a bit short on dollars for other things because of this, but I really want this to happen. It's important to me."

"Does she know about this?"

"No, and I don't want her to know until it's too late to argue. She won't want to take it. She's going to give you a hard time. Give it right back to her. It's a priority. It's necessary. It's long overdue."

"Do I hand it to her in person?"

"No! She lives out of state. It's a long way. Just mail it and follow up with a phone call. Will you do this for me?"

"I will! Should I include a note or anything?"

"No. She'll understand."

"Not that it's any of my business, but can you help me to understand?"

"You're right. It's none of your business."

I didn't pursue the topic any further. That is how our relationship worked. Nothing needed to be explained. We both accepted what was shared and moved on. Some things were never fully talked about, even though they left big and burning questions between us.

Gordon never gave me all the details of the accident that left his friends dead and him a quadriplegic. Only once was he able to briefly cover that subject, but it was too painful for him to relive. I tried to go there, thinking that sharing might help, but that conversational road was closed.

He rarely talked about how he felt regarding death either, but I always thought he feared it down to his very bones. This surprised me since death's presence was so obvious. Also, among his thousands of books could be found religious and philosophy books whose sections on death, dying, and the afterlife were well-worn.

Death wasn't allowed much room in any conversation, especially after my severe stroke that made death relocate to the east coast for a year. When I was finally able to visit Gordon, he only let me give a brief synopsis of my near-death experience. That shared recounting of the event covered the minimal facts. The doctors had not given me much of a chance to survive. I spent a year learning how to walk as well as talk and learned that another stroke was possible at any moment.

I was forty-five at the time of my calamity; Gordon was in his early twenties when he faced death's door. Now we were both senior citizens and different types of time bombs. We didn't speak of it.

Maybe additional words never needed to be said. Even without words, the stroke seemed to have made us closer. Death sat at an equal distance between us both, and we knew it. We had learned that anything is possible at any instant and that we were connected by life, not death.

I had visited Gordon many times over four decades. We knew each other in all stages of our adult lives. At the time of this visit to California, Gordon was in his late sixties, and I had just turned seventy. We had shared thousands of stories between us over the years and hoped to share more. Through those many occasions of sharing, I learned that a story cannot always be told in one sitting and that patience is required. Life's stories, though sequential in their living, can be random in the telling, free from the linear restrictions of time.

Two margaritas later, he began to talk about his nurse. "When I regained consciousness, I wasn't the same person. I couldn't walk! I couldn't move! I couldn't feed myself! I couldn't piss or take a shit! Suddenly, I was mostly paralyzed, dead weight! She was my everything. She fed me. She wiped my ass! More than that, she did it as a woman, not a nurse.

She talked to me. She made me laugh. When she touched my forehead to push back my hair, she made me feel like I was a man. She wouldn't let me see myself as a person with a list of could-nots a mile long. For her, it was all about the list of coulds that she expected me to build and expand upon. Is that enough?"

"More than enough. Thank you. But I would like a little more detail about how she wiped your ass!"

We laughed, which was a big part of our world, finished our drinks, and headed back to his place. I still didn't believe the trips to the lawyer or the will or the list of what was to go where or the big check to his nurse would need to be dealt with. I was wrong!

THE ROAD TRIP

Back in Pennsylvania, a few months later, I was in the kitchen one night when the phone rang. It was Gordon's doctor, calling from the hospital in California. Apparently, Gordon had developed another bladder infection, a raging fever, and pneumonia. He had been rushed to the hospital. The doctor said that the situation didn't look hopeful but that he was going to put Gordon into an induced coma to let his body rest and heal as much as possible during this latest trauma.

The call was cryptic and over with before I could even think of questions I wanted to ask. The doctor promised to let me know of any changes in Gordon's situation and hung up!

Within moments, I was on the phone, trying to get a flight to John Wayne Airport. This was the closest airport to the hospital and one where I knew I could get Gordon's friend, Steve, to pick me up. If I had to fly into LAX, I'd have to rent a car, which isn't cheap, and be further from my destination.

Unfortunately, there were several huge events happening in the Orange County region, and no matter which airline I called or travel agent I reached, I found no available flight options.

"Everything is booked! There are no flights at either airport," I said to my wife, Terry. "I'm going to drive! I have to be there when he comes out of the coma. I can be there in time, if I really push!"

Terry preferred I'd wait for an available flight but understood and helped me pack.

Early the next morning, I was on my way. I checked the national weather report and decided to head south first to avoid some major storms in the center of the country and then take the southern route, west, to Lake Forest, California. It was a long drive, but I was up for it.

In retrospect, it was probably not one of my better ideas, but I didn't realize that until I was several states away. My mind was all over the place with memories of Gordon and decades of shared experiences along with the stories we told each other. I kept drifting into a recollection and come out of it finding myself in another state.

I remembered Gordon telling me how embarrassing it was for him to learn to handle the electric wheelchair.

"I always liked to drive," he said. "I like being in control, and there isn't much I have control over, these days. After months in the hospital and all kinds of physical therapy, the doctors finally believed I was ready for wheels. I attempted to convince my nurse to steal a motorized chair from the equipment room. She wouldn't do it! I even tried bribing her, saying she could sit on my lap, and we could head to a restaurant I'd spotted from my hospital room window."

"Would that be a date," she asked, "or kidnapping?"

"Does it matter?" I asked.

"Well, employees aren't allowed to date patients, but if it's kidnapping, it's out of my hands!"

"Then you'll do it?"

"As much as I'd like to have a little adventure and lunch, I think one of us should exercise a little restraint and follow protocol. First, you go through the electric-wheelchair training and then we'll see."

"But I know how to drive!"

"We'll see," she repeated. "I'll come watch your first lesson."

"Wear something nice. We'll be heading out as soon as the lesson's over!"

"The very next day, they wheeled me to the ground floor for a short video and an explanation of the chair, including how to charge it, how to turn it, how to go forward and backward, and how to adjust speed. I was bored out of my mind! Their details about how I was to be strapped in took over twenty minutes, and they repeated that entire part twice. Finally, they let me sit in the damned thing and made me repeat all the instructions. Eventually, they escorted me through the crowded cafeteria with huge windows that looked out at the rear parking lot where orange cones had been placed in certain patterns to simulate sidewalks, roads, and barriers.

"With my almost date by my side in her red sleeveless dress and sassy smile, the technician gave me the directions and said, 'Go ahead. Show us what you can do!'

"Without going into excruciating detail, I pushed the red lever forward—way forward! In two seconds, I was traveling at the speed of light, going this way and that way on one side and then another of the neatly lined series of cones and obstacles. I was on four wheels and then two wheels and then over on no wheels with an audience of hundreds, including the one person that really mattered."

"Now aren't you glad you learned how important it is to be strapped in properly?" she said once I was safely back in my room with a bump on my head. "Don't worry. You'll get it! By the way, now that I see that you're a pretty fast mover, we might need a chaperone!"

I always meant to write about that story of Gordon's but never seemed to find the time.

HEADING WEST

When I couldn't take the traffic and rumble of the road any longer, I exited, pulled into a fast-food parking lot, and turned off the engine. I cried for a while, alone in the car where no one and nothing could interrupt the sadness that suddenly overwhelmed me. Then I went in and stuffed a grocery bag with enough snack foods to keep me alert for a few more hours.

There's nothing like an overdose of sugar, salt, carbs, and everything that goes into nonessential munchies to graze upon during a road trip. I had chocolate in every form possible, even some with nuts and raisins to pretend a sense of health consciousness. There were a couple of hotdogs, three pieces of pizza, bags of popcorn, potato chips, pretzels, supersized cups of coffee, and eight different types of carbonated drinks to drown in. It all kept me awake, but I wasn't feeling my best.

Sometime after midnight when the need for restroom stops became too frequent, I found a cheap motel next to a bar that featured an array of classic diner foods and popular drinks. I chose to forego their gastronomic delights and settled on drinking supper. I thought it would help me sleep. It was the best idea I'd had all day!

I don't even remember closing my eyes. My last memory was of putting the key in the lock of my weathered motel door. I woke up at five in the morning, still fully dressed and with breath that could have been used as a military weapon.

After checking my cell phone for any medical updates, taking a very necessary shower, and eating an order of bacon and eggs from a seedy joint on the corner, I hit the road, heading west. The southern leg of my journey was behind me, and I had a sense of accomplishment having the sun in my rearview mirror.

It seemed that I was always heading west in a car, on a motorcycle, or in a plane. I used to fly to California with Gordon's sister, Sony, who had been my best friend for years. She had asked me long ago to travel with her to visit Gordon, saying, "I know you guys are going to hit it off." We did, eventually, but in the beginning, Gordon wasn't sold on the idea of Sony bringing a stranger into his world. On the plane ride out to California, Sony confessed that Gordon had called her multiple times to express his concerns and questions about my visit. Sony said the conversations went something like this:

"David will be bored!"

"No, he won't!"

"He'll just see me as a freak."

"Then don't act like one!"

"I live on a time frame totally determined by health-care workers and pills."

"He'll adjust."

"He's used to a lot more activity than what goes on around here."

"He can liven things up a bit."

"What can I talk to him about?"

"Anything! Everything!"

"He's got a job, a wife, and three kids!"

"So what?"

"So we have nothing in common!"

"Find something."

"I'm weak. He's strong."

"So what!"

"He can't come!"

"David already bought his ticket!"

"Fuck! Does he like movies?"

"Loves them!"

"Does he read?"

"Yup, and writes too."

"Well of course he does!"

"Nice sarcasm! And by the way, he studied art in college."

"Motherfucker!"

Sony up and died on me after many years of friendship and many trips to California. Losing her was difficult. She had been a huge part of my life. Gordon lived on, so the connection to Sony was still alive.

I kept going west.

SPOON RIVER

Sony and I had both been cast in a production of *Spoon River Anthology* in 1972. She was a veteran of the stage, and this was my first venture into the theater world. She was five years older than me and had moved east to escape the small town, small mindedness of southwest Texas. She was also escaping from her mother, Wilma, who never escaped her own trap and never tested her artistic talents in a big city. Her mother was an aging beauty who drank too much too often and had a nasty streak fed by the alcohol.

Sony had long wavy black hair, dark eyes, ivory skin, and an amazing intellect! She was once asked if she would be interested in being in the Miss Texas pageant. She declined! Both the invitation and the declining made her mother furious.

In college, Sony had been the treasure of the theater department and star of every production, *Madea* being her all-time favorite. Her mother saw her as competition and criticized her every move, except her move east. It was a love-hate relationship, and sometimes the hate won.

Sony thought she'd audition in New York for Broadway plays. She did, but the money ran out before the parts rolled in, so she took a teaching job to keep her away from Texas and her mother. The job was outside Philly. It was not New York, but the Big Apple was just a train ride away. She soon realized that even the train ride was too far, so she auditioned in the Philly theater scene and soon found herself embracing Philadelphia as her home.

The entire cast of *Spoon River* became incredibly close. The play is a very complicated piece of theater, requiring a small cast to play a wide variety of characters. The play is monologue driven and showcases different relationships as well as philosophies. It also emphasized how each of us live interrelated lives with each other. That was the important lesson that I took from the experience.

The play required hours of strenuous rehearsals that lead to lots of cast parties and great conversations. During one of those conversations, I asked Sony why she never dated. I knew she had many men who were interested and saw her turn them all away.

"It's like this, David. My father and two of my aunts died of early Alzheimer's disease. It's in the family, and I'm not going to inflict that on anyone. I don't want to get so close to someone that my being ill would cause them pain. I also won't pass this genetic jeopardy on to another generation. I've got my job. I've got theater. I've got my writing. I've got friends. That's enough." Sony and I never talked about that situation again.

We talked about and shared everything else, including the desire to travel to far away and exotic places. Money was tight, so we let our writing transport us to imaginary worlds or places we couldn't afford to go. When we became more financially solvent, we did our best to realize those larger travel dreams.

The play resulted in a connection that we both called the Spoon River effect, and we both looked for it everywhere we traveled and in every person we met. I looked for it in Gordon but was originally met with some resistance. He didn't seem to want the connection and perhaps was a little angry that Sony and I had bonded.

YOU CAME BACK

I was always looking for the next road trip or adventure! Being in motion was when I felt most comfortable, especially following times of being relatively contained. When I was fresh out of the Army in 1972 and was twenty-two years old, I took a road trip with a buddy who'd just returned from Vietnam. We were on our way to Virginia Beach, looking for girls and a pathway into civilian life.

While my old friend settled into a local bar for "just a couple of beers," I went to visit Terry, a girl I'd met in college who lived in a small town west of Philadelphia. She was in the middle of packing for her return to Kansas, but we had time to talk and reminisce about college days and college friends. In many ways, I wished I was going with her but never said it out loud.

Before getting back on the highway, I submitted an application for a teaching position at a new high school I'd spotted from the road. The personnel director had an appointment cancelation and offered me the opportunity to interview on the spot, and I jumped for it.

I wasn't quite dressed appropriately for an interview but thought it would be good practice. I needed to start looking for a job soon and needed to sharpen my interview skills.

Because the interview was so unexpected and sudden, I found myself relaxed and even enjoying the process.

It only took about an hour, and I knew my buddy would not mind hanging out at the bar a little longer.

When I got to the bar, I tried telling him all about Terry and the interview, but he fell asleep and stayed that way for most of the trip.

After five days of exploring the Virginia Beach nightlife, swimming, bar hopping, and girl watching, I called home to Syracuse, New York, to let my parents know we'd be heading back north soon.

To my surprise, my mother asked if I'd submitted an application for teaching art outside Philly. By that time, I'd almost forgotten that I had an interview and had filled out all the paperwork for that teaching job. "How'd you know that?" I asked, never expecting to be contacted so soon. "Well, they called. You got the job! You're to report to their central office on August 18," she said with some disappointment in her voice. I'm sure she wanted me to start my career closer to home but that was never my plan. I loved my parents, but I was looking for new horizons, new experiences, and returning to Syracuse wasn't going to work for me.

Included in my plans were promises to myself to take full advantage of being young, to travel, try new things, and discover what I was capable of. I wrote those exact words to Terry after she returned to college for her junior year.

I filled her in on the beginnings of my teaching career along with my struggles to buy used furniture and second-hand kitchen items for the apartment I was renting. I told her that I was surviving mostly on hotdogs, popcorn, and frozen pizza. I also let her know that I had auditioned for a part in a play at a local theater.

I didn't mean to audition! I'd gone to a monthly meeting at the playhouse in an attempt to learn more about the community and make some friends. I signed in at the door and took a seat. Twenty minutes later, they were reading names off that list for tryouts. Too embarrassed to admit what I had done, I awkwardly walked to center stage and read what was handed me.

I had painted sets and designed backdrops for high school productions but had never been on stage before. I tried not to make a fool of myself and read as best as I could under the circumstances, knowing that it would soon be over with, and I'd never see those people again. I wasn't worried about any further repercussions because I never dreamed I'd be cast. When I got the call to come to the first rehearsal, I just about shit my pants.

I told Gordon that story years ago, and he laughed his ass off! He always wanted me to tell him stories about my life and constantly questioned why I didn't write them down. I had planned to write them, but before I could, I'd find myself looking for the next story. Finding stories came easy, but the discipline of sitting down and writing came hard.

Gordon said that I was his scout! My job was to traverse distant territories and then report back to him with tales of my experiences. It became part of our agenda with every visit. The crazier the story, the more he loved it. I suspect it was because his world was extremely quiet and very small.

He wanted to hear all the noise of my life and demanded lots of details. Whenever there was a lag in the conversation, he'd look at me and say, "Well, scout, do you have a story for me?" That was usually just about the time I was getting him ready for his night aide to come on duty.

I'd carry a comfortable chair into his bedroom, park it next to his wheelchair, and share some account connected to my life. Sometimes he'd direct the genre of the story and say, "Make it a funny one," and I would. Each story would usually take about an hour, including time for his many questions. I always tried to wrap it up by the time his aide came to put him into bed. Then I would go to my room, lay down, and close my eyes. I never slept until long after the aide was gone. I didn't sleep because I could hear Gordon laugh periodically as he lay in bed recounting the story I'd told him. Hearing him laugh was better than sleep!

Visiting Gordon became a regular event for me, but no matter how often I visited, Gordon always greeted me the same way—with surprise!

"You came back!"

"I told you I would! Now what adventure should we plan?"

There would be no adventure to plan this time. Gordon had no idea that I was on my way to him, and I had no idea if he would be there when I arrived.

I called the hospital again and was told that the doctor was with Gordon at the moment. The nurse said, "The doctor will call you as soon as the current crisis is over."

I tried to get her to explain the details of the crisis that was on top of a prior crisis but was told, "The doctor is the only one that can answer your questions!"

I continued to drive but kept my phone within easy reach while memories took my head far away, catching a story line temporarily and keeping me from facing thoughts of Gordon's coma.

THE PASSPORT

As our kids got a little older, my wife would join me for a visit. I didn't give Gordon a heads-up regarding Terry's coming, knowing how he had reacted to my first visit. He had met her once when he traveled east with an aide, and I thought that was enough. I was sure they'd find common interests, and they did! Terry shared Gordon's love of books, art history, and museums. Terry became Gordon's pen pal and wrote to him frequently. He especially loved it when my wife and I went hiking in Europe. He saved each letter and postcard, sharing them with his few friends and health-care workers.

Terry and I had talked about the possibility of getting Gordon to Paris. He knew about everything that was in the Louvre and the other great museums of that famous city. Gordon was totally into the idea of an international trip and insisted we get his passport updated. Unfortunately, we had to drop that dream following his trip to the East Coast and having to face the realities of traveling with someone as fragile as my friend.

Nothing was easy. A place to empty his urine bag was not always available. Doors were not always wide enough for his wheelchair, and some restaurants wouldn't seat us because "Your friend's situation makes our other guests feel uncomfortable." He needed air-conditioning but couldn't have the air blowing directly on him. He got tired easily and needed me to adjust him in his chair every twenty minutes. Some places had no ramps or elevators, and many sidewalks were too busted up to maneuver.

I had to be on constant alert to everything. Has he had enough water? Is he overtired? Is he getting a bedsore? Is he tied down in the van properly? Has he had the right medications at the right times? Has he eaten his fruit today? Does he have a fever? Is he having a good time?

That last question was the only one to which I was sure of the correct answer. He loved it all! He loved Philadelphia and its famous South Street. He loved Gettysburg and its history. He loved Baltimore and the Inner Harbor. He loved New York City and Broadway. He loved everything, and we loved taking him to those places, but it was exhausting and at times, scary.

When we got Gordon and his aide on to the plane and returned the access van along with the rented hospital bed, Terry, Sony, and I collapsed, realizing that taking Gordon to Europe was out of the question. We settled for more regular trips to California and destinations within an hour and a half of his home. It wasn't Paris, but it would do. I did get Gordon's photograph taken to send in with his passport application. Even the idea of having a passport excited him and allowed him to imagine a future, which included greater adventures. When it came in the mail, he displayed it, like it was a trophy.

GORDON'S FAVORITE STORY

While trying and failing to keep my mind on the road, I thought about the one story I told Gordon that he would ask me to tell again and again.

He'd say, "Tell me how you asked Terry to marry you!"

I'd shake my head, saying, "You already heard that a thousand times."

"It's your fault! If you'd just sit still long enough to write the story, I wouldn't have to beg you to tell it! Why haven't you done that?"

"I've been busy."

"Then get busy telling me the story! Tell it from the beginning and no shortcuts."

I'd try to interest him in some sort of mystery or adventure or time in the Army or crazy things that happened in the classroom or travels, but more often than not, I'd tell that story.

"I give up. But this is the last time!"

I always said that, but I always told it again.

"It was like this. My parents were visiting for the weekend. I had cleaned the spare room for them upstairs and was still trying to tidy up the living room while they were unpacking. I told them that I had planned a date for that night when they called to see if this particular weekend was available but that didn't matter. They said they'd just sit on the porch or maybe watch a little TV while I was gone.

"In the middle of trying to make the place look respectable, I heard a car come down the stone lane that lead to the old farmhouse, half of which I rented. I moved there once the lease was up on my apartment in an attempt to save money and get out in the country.

"It was Terry! She had met my parents many times and was stopping by after work to say hello. Her summer job was working in an unair-conditioned sweatshop, making draperies. She had hoped to get something related to her major, but jobs in the art world are always at a premium. Terry burst through the door and scanned the room for my folks."

"Where are they?"

"Unpacking and washing up a bit. What's your hurry?"

"I've got a date tonight, and I have to get home to wash my hair."

"Is it Ralph again?"

"Why do you say it like that?"

"Like what?"

"You know, like you were referring to a stray dog."

"Sorry!"

"He's not so bad, you know."

"I said I'm sorry!"

"And what are you doing tonight? Are you still going out with—"

"Yes," I interrupted to prevent her from sabotaging my date's name.

"I wish your parents would hurry up. I can't go out looking like this," she said while pulling at her long brown hair.

"They'll be awhile. Why don't you wash it here in the kitchen sink? I've got some extra towels in the bottom of that cabinet."

"Good idea," she said while rolling up her sleeves and tucking in the collar of her blouse.

"I just bought some shampoo today. It's in that bag on the counter."

"It's not going to make me smell like Old Spice, is it?"

"Does it matter?"

"It might! You don't like Ralph, do you?" was the last thing she said before lathering up under the faucet.

It wasn't unusual for me to see Terry wash her hair. During the summer of 1974, Terry, Sony, and I backpacked for seven weeks all over Europe and even went to Egypt. We were used to seeing each other in unflattering ways.

We did the trip on a shoestring budget, sleeping outside in construction sites, parks, graveyards, and on trains. We had no money for extras. I had only been teaching for a couple of years, and my salary barely covered the essentials. Sony was a little more financially secure and even had a credit card! Terry had just graduated from college. The only thing she had was a student loan. Sony called her mother and asked if she would lend Terry the money for the trip, and to our surprise, she did. Sony always suspected her mother sent the money because Wilma didn't want her daughter running all over Europe without another woman along. She also knew her mother had always dreamed of going to Europe herself. The trip was a great adventure, which bonded the three of us together forever.

All of a sudden, she was done. She wrapped her wet hair up in a white towel and turned to me for an answer to her last question.

"Well?"

"Ralph's all right, but—"

"But what?"

I just stared at her, standing there, dripping wet without a trace of makeup and full of attitude, and the answer suddenly came to me.

"But I think you should marry me!"

"When?" she instantly questioned.

"As soon as possible before I change my mind," I said, grabbing her arm and pulling her to the bottom of the stairs as I called for my parents who both appeared at the top at the same time.

"What do you think about the two of us getting married?"

"Sounds like a good idea," my father shouted with my mother agreeing.

Privately, out on the porch later that night, my father wanted a few details.

"I think she's great, and I couldn't be happier for the both of you. You've known Terry a long time, and well, I thought that maybe you were just friends. Now out of the blue, you're going to get married. Is it because she's pretty and smart? Is it because she likes travel and adventure? Is it because she's sweet and likes a good laugh? After all this time, what made you decide?"

"Her lips, Dad. I couldn't stand the thought of anybody else kissing those beautiful lips."

He put his arm around my shoulders, saying, "Now that I understand!"

Seven weeks later, Terry and I were married!

"Jesus, I love that story," Gordon blurted out. "Were you ever sorry you took the plunge?"

"My only regret is that I shared the story with you."

Twenty minutes after the aide left, as I lay awake in my bed, I heard Gordon laugh and whisper, "Those beautiful lips."

I thought about those lips on that trip to California and tried to get my head to a different place.

I smartened up and was taking regular breaks to get out from behind the wheel and drink water. I found myself unable to stop picturing Gordon in a coma. I wondered if within his medically induced sleep, he was living out one of my stories or perhaps one of our day trips to LA or Laguna Beach or Big Bear Mountain. I prayed he was not reliving the accident!

BIG BEAR MOUNTAIN

Our trip to Big Bear was one of our last big outings. Terry and I were both in California, and we thought that despite his declining physical strength, with the two of us, we could make the trip happen. Gordon was excited about going and seeing a different landscape other than the suburban sprawl of Lake Forest. He lived in a nice middle-class neighborhood of one- and two-story houses and ranchers with well-tended yards in a wooded area with lots of shade. It was close to shopping, banks, medical facilities, schools, and a few good restaurants.

Gordon bought the place in 1974 with assistance from the government since he was still in the Navy at the time of the accident. As a veteran, he was able to afford all kinds of services that that allowed him to live a relatively independent life, even with his disabilities. He rented out one bedroom to a single man who was there at night in case of emergencies.

Gordon also had an aide that came in the morning to get him out of bed, showered, fed, and into his wheelchair. At night, another aide came to do the process in reverse. In between those two medically inspired human interactions were hours and hours and hours of loneliness.

Gordon filled his time with books and television and music. Eventually, after he bought and learned to operate a modified van, there were regular trips to Irvine where he went to college. He graduated at the head of his class and found purpose while taking an art course, inspiring him to attempt pencil drawing. It wasn't easy but then again, nothing was easy! His mother had been an artist, but Gordon had never even considered picking up a pencil to draw until it seemed an impossible thing to do.

We packed the van with all the necessary medical and emergency things plus extra clothes, pillows, water bottles, sunglasses, hats, cell phones, ramps, snacks, cameras, rags, paper towels, Lysol disinfectant, flashlights, and an array of various other things in an attempt to be ready for anything.

After filling up with gas and checking tire pressure, we were off to Big Bear Mountain. It took forever to get beyond the superhighways, housing sprawl, and past shopping mall after shopping mall after shopping mall, each comprised of the same collection of big-box stores and fast-food chains.

The traffic was unbearable, but all I kept thinking about was that this is for Gordon. Then the scent of ripe urine began to waft up and circulate though the van's air-conditioning system. It stung my eyes and made my nose run. I wondered if Gordon had become aware of the stench and possible mess on his clothes and in the van. He cared a great deal about how he looked and was particular about appearing and smelling as normal and healthy as possible.

It had taken him twenty minutes to choose the right outfit for the day, and I knew he would be mortified if something had gone wrong with his tubing and urine was leaking out and into his new jeans and across the van's floor. Urine by itself has a distinctive and pungent aroma, add to that the number of medications that Gordon was taking, and the result is pretty staggering. Before he could comment, I pulled into a gas station, saying I wanted to clean the windshield.

"I'll open up the car to let some fresh air in while I'm scrubbing the dead bugs off."

When I slid back the rear door, the puddle of urine was already breaking over the raised edge of the rubber floor mat and soaking into the rug. Gordon had become nose blind to the smell of urine over the years, and I didn't think he was fully conscious of the extent of our current situation.

"Since we're already stopped, why don't I get you out and empty your urine bag before we go on to the park?"

"Sounds good, Dave. I need to get repositioned in this chair anyway."

While checking the tubing that ran up his pants to his catheter, I discovered a long crack, just above the top of his sock. It took some time, but I figured a way to cut that section out and reposition the drainage port a little higher up on his leg. Then I motioned for Terry to join us at the woods edge.

Terry came quickly and kept him occupied in conversation while I returned to the van. I soaked up urine, disposed of the evidence, and sprayed the hell out of the vehicle. It really didn't smell much better, but it did give us something different to choke on. Just as I finished locking Gordon back in place, he looked at me and said, "Thanks, Dave. Sorry I'm so much trouble."

"Don't worry about it, Gordon! What's a little piss among friends?" He shot me a quick smile before the door clicked shut.

It started to rain as we entered the park, but it didn't matter to anyone. Even the rain was a treat for a guy living in southern California. He thought it was great and put the entire urine incident behind him, which allowed us to do the same. Within minutes, we were absorbed in conversation about mountain views and the different vegetation and appreciation of the natural world.

Eventually, the topic of lunch became the center of our discussion, and I began to look for an appropriate place to grab a bite to eat. Of course, this place had to meet certain criteria. First of all, there had to be outside seating. The bottom of Gordon's pants still smelled of urine, and though the three of us were trying not to notice, other people would.

We also needed a place where I could park and help Gordon exit through the door on the side of the van once I'd fully extended the ramp. Many times, the parking spots for the handicapped were used by the physically able with no consideration for someone in Gordon's condition. I'd get all pissed off, and Gordon would just say, "Fuck 'em! They can't understand because all of this is outside their world of experience. They can't picture this, so fuck 'em."

Fortunately, we found a country store that had outside picnic tables protected by big yellow umbrellas. It wasn't fine dining, but they had great hamburgers and cold beer from a local brewery. It worked, and once I got Gordon positioned at the end of the table, we were greeted by the owner who treated us like long-lost relatives and told us stories about mountain bears and coyotes that howled at the moon.

"If you breakdown after dark in these parts, just stay in your vehicle. There are critters around here that are looking to grab a bite, just like you did."

We all laughed, but his words did remind us that we had hours to drive before getting back to Lake Forest and that Gordon's aide was arriving at nine. It poured all the way back, and for some reason, I ran out of words for a conversation. Terry fell asleep first and then Gordon. I cracked open a window to prevent it from happening to me.

We pulled into his development, just as the night aide arrived. I was too tired to tell any stories, and Gordon was too tired to listen. I think I was asleep before the aide left. Despite everything, Gordon's adventure had been a success. The urine incident was forgotten, the scenery was great, the food was good, and we weren't eaten by bears.

FAMILY TRIPS

Sony would have loved our adventure at Big Bear Mountain. Actually, Sony loved going anywhere at any time, just like her brother.

Terry and I made Sony a part of the family. She was in our home for every event, including birthday parties for our three sons, piano recitals, holidays, picnics, and everything else.

We would often take a road trip south over Easter break to escape the winter snow and find a patch of beach where we could build sandcastles with the kids.

Savannah, Georgia, was our favorite getaway. Tybee Island is connected to the mainland by a series of small bridges, and there, we rented a small place on the beach. It cost 110 dollars for the week and included a small kitchen. It was pretty much a dump, but we didn't care.

Our extended family also visited upstate New York and multiple local places of interest. Pennsylvania is loaded with historic sites, parks, trails, rivers, lakes, and mountains.

There were many places to go and things to do that didn't cost a dime. We took advantage of every single one with lots of spontaneous excursions thrown together on the spot, just because the sun was shining, and we were in the mood.

We also went to places that took a bit of money and a lot of planning!

When my sons turned four and when they turned fourteen, I took each, one at a time, backpacking in Europe. Terry would stay home to watch the other two kids, traveling with cousins or girlfriends when I was available to watch over the house and all three boys.

Terry and I believed that travel was a necessary part of a child's education and prioritized this in our vacation account and financial strategy.

I was used to part-time jobs and squeezing the budget. Some of those jobs included carpentry work, selling vacuum cleaners, painting murals, singing at weddings or funerals, dancing on stage, and keynoting at writers' conferences.

We also saved a lot of money through bartering. I painted many pieces for dental work and even paid the medical fees for our oldest son's birth by painting a large mural for the doctor's office.

Once, I traded some original designs for a grand piano as a surprise for Terry.

My mother always told me, "Where there's a will, there's a way." She was right!

We did without lots of things in order to afford traveling on the cheap. This gave us a wealth of experiences!

One of the most difficult things I did to increase our income was leaving my teaching position. I loved my job as chairman of the art department but hated all the necessary part-time work that kept me from the family.

Terry and I put our résumés together and applied for a single job that both of us were qualified to do. They hired us at this advertising and printing company for double my teaching pay. As long as the job got done, we could split the workload up any way we liked. It was a win-win for everybody and made our bigger travel plans more possible, especially the ones with the kids.

Sometimes Sony would fly to Europe and meet me and one of the boys to be a part of the adventure.

Often, she would join us in Greece where she would put on her teacher's hat and share her immense knowledge of Greek mythology.

Over the years, she joined us in Austria, France, Hungary, Switzerland, Crete, and many other places.

She was family of choice, and it worked for all of us.

I was lost in thoughts of those travels when my cell phone rang. I overanxiously reached for the phone, shoving it beyond my reach on the car's floor.

Quickly, I pulled to the shoulder, retrieved the phone, and called the doctor.

"David, Gordon's blood pressure is almost nonexistent. I've tried small injections to raise it, but even the tiniest amount of medication results in his blood pressure going sky high. This puts him in danger of coming out of the coma too quickly, resulting in a stroke, heart attack, or brain damage."

"What can be done?" I asked, hearing the urgency in his voice.

"The staff and I are doing everything possible. Gordon is being monitored constantly. I'm going back in with him now."

"Tell him I'm on my way!"

"He can't hear me."

"Tell him anyway, please."

"Tell him his brother is on the way!"

"I will," the doctor promised.

I pulled back onto the highway and into memories.

THE EDWARDIAN EXPERIENCE

On one of our anniversaries, Terry and I met Sony at an airport outside Paris, following a week filled with art museums, Monet's garden, and the café scene. Terry was heading back home while Sony and I were flying off to London for a week of packing as many West End theatre productions into our lives as possible.

With the anniversary and everything else, I hadn't even thought of getting a room in London. When Sony and I were at Victoria station, I spotted a sign advertising Traveler's Aid. I stood in line forever, listening to the London tourist spokeswoman explain to other stranded travelers that "It's the height of the tourist season! Everything is booked!"

She wore a tailored navy-blue suit, a string of pearls with matching earrings, and a smile as fake as the jewelry. Her hair was up in a French twist, and I could smell her perfume from twenty feet away.

When it was finally my turn, I tapped into my acting background, approaching the counter like I owned it. I didn't wait for the monologue I'd heard delivered multiple times over the last thirty minutes. I leaned in on my elbow and took a deep breath, keeping unbreakable eye contact and projecting all the confidence I could muster. Then without giving her an opening, I presented my case, like Perry Mason, addressing the judge in a courtroom drama, recounting the facts, and questioning their supposed legitimacy.

"I know everything is booked! I know that nothing is available within an hour of the city! I know that even the most expensive places have been locked up for months!" I leaned in closer. "But you don't know the wide range of circumstances, which we are willing to tolerate just to stay in the heart of the theater district for a week! Surely, with your vast expertise in the realm of accommodations, there is some special circumstance somewhere that would provide us with shelter during these desperate times."

She burst into laughter and then tried to recompose. I suspect my over-the-top demeanor had thrown her off her game, and she scrambled to get back on script.

"You're an American want-to-be actor on the loose in London," she accused.

"You guessed it, sister! Were you moved by my performance?"

"To tears," she replied, still stifling a smile while opening a drawer and pulling out a single piece of gold-trimmed paper. "Can you tolerate the smell of paint?"

"I'm an artist. I love the smell of paint!"

"Noise? Hammers? Saws? Occasional vulgar language?"

"Fuck yeah!"

She laughed out loud, leaned in so we were elbow to elbow, and whispered, "There's a great hotel that's being refurbished near the theater district. Remember it's all under construction! They'll only rent if you sign this waiver. Are you interested?"

"Do you have a pen?"

"You really are Americans, I presume."

"You presume correctly. We are Americans who love your accent, fish and chips, and theater!"

"Well, Yankee boy, you are also going to love the accommodations. Give this signed waiver to the desk clerk at the Edwardian Hotel. The directions are printed on this paper. It's one of the most prestigious hotels in all of London, but it's being renovated. When the work is finished, the cheapest rooms will rent for five hundred American dollars a night, but right now, three hundred smackers, and it's yours for a week."

"Sounds fantastic," I said while grabbing the waiver. "Thanks for this great welcome to London."

"And I thank you for the performance. I can't give you a Tony Award, so you will have to accept the waiver as my positive theatrical review. Just don't blame me if you can't get a good night's sleep!"

"Believe me. We can sleep anywhere!"

In just a few minutes, we were following the directions through the busy London sidewalks, laughing over what had just happened, and saying how Gordon will love the story.

"I can't believe you pulled that off," Sony shouted over the noise of a double-decker bus, and bustling crowd. "One minute, we're stranded with sleeping on the street our only prospect. The next thing I know, we're staying in one of the finest hotels in London. I don't know how you do it!"

"I didn't do anything more than listen and make her laugh."

"Not everybody listens these days, and making people laugh is a gift. Time with you always has a little magic in it. You made our problem disappear, and the Edwardian come out of nowhere," she said as the doorman in a top hat ushered us to our home for the week.

The place was far beyond our wildest expectations. The clerk took our waiver and our passports after looking us up and down to assess our fiscal and social reliability.

Then he called for a bellboy to take our bags to the second floor. Everything was polished brass and oak. There was a cigar lounge, Victorian bar, antique porcelain globes with fresh flowers on every flat surface, and chandeliers straight from Italy. The floors were marble and rugs, oriental. It was entirely posh and nothing like anything I'd ever experienced before.

We immediately felt underdressed and overly spoiled to have lucked into this treasure. The room was equally spectacular with fresh fruit on the table next to crystal glasses, a bottle of red wine, and chocolates on the pillows. There was also a list of all the shows currently playing in London and phone numbers for each box office. Within an hour, we were showered, dressed in our finest clothes, and headed out for our first play.

We had reserved tickets for a production of *Blood Brothers* written by Willy Russell, a work based on the idea of twins separated at birth. One boy was raised by the ill-equipped and poor birth mother, and the other boy was raised by an upper-class couple where wealth and opportunities were abundant. The twins meet as young men, resulting in friendship, then jealousy and eventual tragedy. Sony and I cried our eyes out for every character. We realized that coming to London was the best thing possible for two actors and aspiring writers who would need to know how to express strong emotions under difficult circumstances.

COOL STREAM

I was deep into Texas before even realizing Arkansas was behind me. I couldn't account for the hundreds of miles I'd already driven. There were vague memories of road signs, mile markers, and pit stops but not much more. The reality of being so out of touch with my surroundings prompted me to pull off the highway and find a place where I could take a walk.

Within a few miles on a country road, I found a small café. I parked there and walked along a dirt path next to a swiftly running stream. It felt good to be going so much slower than the water. It helped me to calm down and detach myself from the race I'd been in.

There was a deeper pool where the stream slowed as it turned and flowed under a bridge. Here, I sat on a log at the water's edge. I kicked off my shoes and pealed down my sweaty socks. They were stuck to my feet, like a set of second skin, resisting my tugging. Rolling up my pant legs, I waded into the cool clear water, watching my toes beneath the rippling surface.

Without the roar of the motor, I could hear my breathing slow down to a recognizable pace. There was a cluster of little white butterflies around some wildflowers at the water's edge. They were up and down and around and over and under each petal and leaf, landing for a moment and then off again without reason.

They reminded me of how I lived before I married Terry. She brought purpose and direction to my existence. I suddenly missed her and the kids very much. The family grounded me in a very positive way, providing me with a place to land and a reason for being. Terry knew me, trusted me, loved me, and let me fly with no doubt I'd return, and I loved her all the more for a freedom I did not feel as a child.

I'd grown up in a home where extra money was rare, but love was abundant. I was the middle child between two girls. Being born in 1948 meant that as the only boy, I was raised to be the responsible one. I was the one who looked after my little sister, and I was the one who mowed the lawn and shoveled the driveway and went to work at an early age to buy the extras that my father's bus driving job could not afford.

I did even more following my mother's operation for cancer. Then as my father took on other part-time jobs, I took care of my mother as best I could. I wanted to! I loved her. I knew it was expected of me, and I complied.

But I also wanted to run away. I could hear the other guys in the neighborhood playing in the street, and I wanted to play too. I wanted to hop on my bike and ride so far that I wouldn't hear my mother calling me from her darkened bedroom. I didn't want to always be the one with the cold compress and pills. Relatives would often pat me on the head and say, "You're a good boy." Sometimes I didn't want to be, but the pattern had already been established. I learned to grab moments between what had to be done, to do the unexpected, and it helped me to survive.

I waded in that cool refreshing water for almost two hours before returning to the car. The café had closed, and the sun was setting.

Even though I'd not put on as many miles as hoped, I was ready for night to fall. The stream had washed me clean and left me in need of sleep. I drove into the little town five miles away, grabbed a bite to eat and a cheap motel room. I quickly fell sound asleep and dreamed of my mother.

My First Motorcycle

Once, during one of my mother's times of remission, I took her shopping at a local mall. On our way back to my very used 1960 Ford Falcon, we passed a motorcycle shop. I paused for moment to look at the shiny deep-blue new model in the shop's huge plate-glass window. It had a large black leather seat and an engine with lots of chrome details.

"What's caught your eye?" my mother asked, and I pointed to the object of my desire.

"I'd love to have a motorcycle! I know I already have that old Ford, but this would be fun."

"Then buy it," she replied.

Her words shocked me and made me laugh at the same time. "No, I can't! There are lots of things we need at home more than a motorcycle."

She turned and walked back to me, taking the bags of recent purchases from my arms. "Can you afford it?"

"Yes, but—"

"But nothing! Honey, if there is one thing this cancer has taught me, it's that you've got to grab every opportunity while you can. You cannot possibly understand how quickly youth slips away. Let's put these things in the car and go check out that blue machine."

Moments later, we were in the showroom, and my mother was asking the salesman more questions than I could think of.

"He'd need a special license, right?"

"Yes, ma'am. In this state, you first have to drive the bike with an experienced motorcyclist sitting behind you for a number of hours. Then you have to pass a test before you can drive on your own."

"Well, that ends this fantasy," I blurted out. "I don't know a single person with a motorcycle license."

"Sure you do," my mother contradicted while rummaging through her purse. "Me," my mother said proudly as she pulled out her wallet and showed us both her license. "My brothers had motorcycles. When I was about seventeen, I got my license so I could ride with them."

I was astonished. No, I was flabbergasted! Within an hour, I'd purchased the blue bike and two white helmets. We left my junker to be picked up later and took the bike out for a two-hour ride.

Along the way, she taught me everything she knew about how to lean on a curve, how to brake, how to use the clutch and shift gears, and how to be safe on the road.

I'd never experienced this side of my mother before. It was better than the motorcycle itself. Within a month, I had my license, remission had faded, and my mother was back in her room. But from that time on, she knew that I knew her.

When I told that story to Gordon, he turned his head into the pillow and quietly wept, saying, "Don't ever tell me that story again."

I didn't ask why.

A MATTER OF PERSPECTIVE

I was dreaming of that cool stream I'd wadded in and butter-flies when I woke to the sound of the trash truck compacting the rubbish outside my room. It was only four thirty in the morning, but I was anxious to get on the road. I checked my phone for messages of which there were none. Minutes later, I was in the car and headed in the wrong direction!

It took a few miles before seeing where the sun was breaking the horizon to realize what I had done. It reminded me of a time when I was in college.

A friend of mine and I were taking a road trip though Colorado on all the twisting back roads we could find. We wanted to experience the winding stretches of pavement that clung to the mountainsides, providing us with thousands of unforgettable views.

We stopped for gas and breakfast, then got back in the car and drove for five hours only to stop at the same place for lunch. We went in to the diner to get a hamburger and some fries and were waited on by the same sassy waitress who served us that morning.

I told her what we'd done, and she said, "Getting lost is a matter of perspective. You can't get lost if you don't care where you're going!"

That memory made me smile.

There have been times in my life when being lost resulted in a greater adventure and absolute surprises. Those were usually the times when my being lost was part of the plan, allowing me to discover a destination that was not even on the map until I arrived.

Being lost can be productive, freeing, exhilarating, and fun! Being lost on purpose and by choice is like having a tool to open up your mind to possibilities that you didn't know existed.

When being lost is totally out of one's control, it can be a weapon that destroys, restricts, and depresses.

I've had being lost both ways!

Sometimes when I take a walk, I just walk with no plan at all.

Sometimes when I sit to paint, or write, I want my head to be as blank as an empty canvas, or a fresh piece of paper. There are times when this works and times when I end up with nothing. It's a chance I sometimes choose to take.

Being lost and having to find my way has given me great joy and profound sadness. It has also provided me with one of my life's greatest lessons.

This time, I really wasn't lost at all, just turned around. I got reoriented and headed west. I knew where I was going and felt that Gordon was waiting for me.

I was hours behind where I'd hoped to be, but I felt more in control and safer, following the break. The stream, the meal, and the good night's sleep had done wonders. As I pulled back onto the highway, I began to think about how Gordon did not want his mother to visit him in the hospital after his accident and wondered if he would want me there now.

THE ACCIDENT

Years ago, late on a Saturday night, Sony's phone rang during a small party with a few teacher friends. That's how she got the news regarding Gordon's accident back in the early seventies.

It was Sony's mother! She had been drinking. Gordon's commanding officer had called Gordon's mother and she in turn had called Sony. Sony couldn't talk to Gordon because he was still unconscious and in critical condition, but Sony didn't need to. She knew Gordon would not want his mother to fly to his bedside.

Wilma would be too dramatic, overreact to his injuries, cause a scene at the hospital, and get drunk. She had a habit of making everything about herself, and this particular tragic event was about Gordon.

Fortunately, Sony went to California, so none of those feared behaviors came to pass. When Gordon woke, the most important person in his life was there for him.

It seems impossible, but I was not even in the picture at that point, so Sony had to tackle that on her own.

Now years of stories and adventures later, Wilma and Sony were both dead along with dozens of my old friends from college and work and theater and travels.

I was left with the hope of being everything Gordon needed because there was no one else.

I wanted him to live. I wanted him to tell me more of his stories, and I wanted to tell him more of mine.

Somehow having someone in this world who knows your stories makes life more real, confirming it's not just a dream or something you imagined.

I can remember my father telling me years ago how difficult it was to have old friends die.

"It's like having part of yourself die," he repeated twice as if hearing it twice would make me understand.

I didn't because I was still too young, but eventually, I understood by living long enough.

He was ninety-two at the time and had seen death from all angles. He told me about his landing on Omaha Beach during the D-Day invasion. "As soon as I dragged myself onto the shore, the only thing that kept me moving forward was my orders. Everything else had completely gone out of my head.

"The noise was deafening! I was surrounded by tanks and artillery and thousands of men crawling through blood-soaked sand. Rifle fire and machine guns filled the air with screaming bullets while grenades and land mines blew body parts in every direction.

"I kept my face down, crawling under barbed wire, grinding the skin off my nose and hands as I body surfed into the position I was to hold. Once there, I pulled my rifle up to my shoulder, leaned into the site, and pulled the trigger again and again as I had been trained.

"It smelled of diesel, gunpowder, and urine. There was smoke everywhere. I could hardly see anything but the ridgeline where the enemy hid in their concrete bunkers. I heard the roar of bombers and calls for medics as one dying soldier fell beside me, crying for his mother.

"Many hours later, I stood in the aftermath of hell to see the tailgate of a truck, carrying my dead comrades, break open, spilling its load, bodies rolling back down to the water's edge.

"I was alive and found it hard to believe. I couldn't move. I didn't know what to do until I heard the order."

"Sergeant, restack those bodies on that truck!"

"I carried out the order, calling each man's name as I read their dog tag. Some I knew. Most I didn't, but they were all brothers to me.

"After the war, those that survived told the story to each other and those that would listen, but only those who were really there could understand.

"As more veterans died, the less the story was told. That's why I'm telling you, David. Try to remember! Tell the story for me!"

"I will, Dad. I promise," I whispered.

"I no longer know a single living soul that was there that day. Who can I tell the story to that still hears the order to charge ringing in their ears?

"A few of us lived to grow old, but one by one, we all fall back on that beach. No matter where you bury me, that's where I'll be."

When I told that story to Gordon, he said, "You must write down what your father shared with you. None of us are going to live forever, and those words have to live on. I've spent a lot of time in the Veteran's Hospital, and the war stories have left me with one thought. War is a planned accident that unfolds in slow motion, killing, scarring, injuring, disabling, and laying the groundwork for the next war. Pass those words on to the next generation while you're at it."

I'll Have the Special

I drove for miles with the windows open. The sun was barely up, and the air was cool and refreshing. For some reason, my prayer for Gordon's recovery was renewed, and I felt energized by the freedom of the road. I didn't realize I'd missed breakfast until I started to feel hungry for lunch.

I passed by lots of nationally known and franchised eateries, preferring locally owned and operated places where the people and food seemed more real. In most cases, this means getting a few miles away from the highway, and even though this cost time, it always resulted in gaining some experience and perhaps another story for Gordon. I sucked down water and snacked on pretzels for a few hours and then had to look for a place for food and gas.

I came across a region of small farms and saw signs advertising Mom's barbecue. The place was a throwback to another time. A time before the highway and before restaurants were inspected and required to meet certain standards of health and cleanliness. There was an old and unpainted wooden front porch that shook as I walked up the steps and pulled open the screen door that had no screen.

"Grab a chair, sonny," a voice shouted out from behind the counter where she was tending the grill in a cloud of smoke. "Make sure it's one that can take your weight," she continued with her back to me. "I had a customer in here last week who must have weighed three hundred pounds. He dropped down like a sack of feed, and all four chair legs did the splits."

I pushed the crumbs off the table and sat as she came out to take my order.

"We got a special on today: a tasty barbecue sandwich and apple pie. That's it, sweet cakes! If you're around tomorrow, the special includes a pickle. The day after that, you'll get a slice of tomato. I don't let too much change around here."

She looked as if she had worked there for the last hundred years and had worn the same apron the entire time. Her face had been roasted in the Texas sun, framing her light-blue eyes in a rugged landscape of wrinkles on wrinkles.

"Well, sweetheart, I'll just have to have the special!"

"I thought you might," she said with a wink and a smile that pulled the lines in her face into a coordinated masterpiece of joy, and I smiled back.

"I'll have to give you a double order of dessert for that smile, honey. Besides, you could use a little fat on that scrawny ass."

I laughed and questioned, "Scrawny ass? How would you know? I'm sitting on it!"

"I heard your footsteps on those stairs. I don't need to see your ass. I don't even want to see your ass. That boat has sailed! You've got a light step. Even when you crossed the floor, nothing squeaked. You walk like a dancer, turning on your toes, confident and sure footed, not like the shit-covered cowboy boots that crash through here every day. You're not gay, are you?"

I laughed again at her forthright, unfiltered approach to conversation.

"No, I'm not gay. Would it matter?"

"No," she continued while returning behind the counter. "I'm trying to find a man for my great-granddaughter, and I think she'd prefer one that would get an erection over her and not the milkman."

"I like your style," I laughed. "I'm from Philadelphia, and I don't get to hear talk that hasn't been premeditated, analyzed, and delivered for a specific effect."

"Here's lunch, city boy. The coffee's on the house," she said, sliding everything across the table. "I talk like me because I don't have a television, and I don't go to the movies. I'm an original. I don't pretend to be anything or anybody. My style, as you put it, is authentic. I am an original, and I plan on staying this way."

"Is your great-granddaughter an original also?"

"Hell no! She looks just like the cover of a fashion magazine and sounds like a television taught her how to talk. Don't get me wrong. She's a good girl, but she's a copy, like so many other copies. It's the tragedy of this generation. She can't help it. It's how it is until something else takes its place. Now eat up before it gets cold. I'd like you to get more of that food than the flies!"

I left ten dollars on the table before crossing to the door.

I heard Mom shout as I walked down the steps, "Sounds like a dancer to me."

DANCING

After gassing up, I rejoined the race. Traffic was thick and even the tandem trucks were passing me, irritated that I wasn't up to speed. I got there, but it took a while, not because of the car but because my internal drive had been temporarily modified by my visit to Mom's barbecue.

I liked her one-of-a-kind attitude. Her life as well as her restaurant was off the beaten track. The way she read my footsteps as that of a dancer reminded me of how Sherlock Holmes deduced any number of facts from a stain on someone's lapel to a cigarette ash on the windowsill. It's as if everything says something about something, and almost nobody is listening. I found it fascinating that Mom saw something in me that so many others had missed or misunderstood.

My life had been heavily influenced by dance. My parents met at a USO dance in Worcester, Massachusetts, in 1940, just prior to my father being deployed overseas. They exchanged addresses after one dance. Over the next five years, they corresponded as he and the First Division fought the war from North Africa to Europe.

My mother worked in a factory, lived at home, and continued sending and receiving letters. Eventually, one of these letters included a proposal. The war ended, my father returned home, and there was a wedding. At the reception, they danced. It was the first time they had danced together since the USO, and though the beat changed many times, they kept dancing.

I've told that story hundreds of times. People always say: "So romantic," "Fascinating," and "Love at first sight!" My favorite response is "That must have been one hell of a dance!" I suppose it was.

Most people change partners many times over a lifetime, looking for someone or some cause to move in unison with as they negotiate the twists and turns of this dance. How can any of us know who or what to stick with until the music's over? How do we know if what we're in step with will make us whole or kill us?

Gordon told me he never danced, even though he wanted to.

"Long before I was tied to this chair, I was afraid to try. I never learned. I watched! I'd strike a cool pose on the edge of the dance floor and be as still as possible. Almost invisible!

"I've always loved music, all different kinds of music, but I never knew how to move to it, and that not knowing made me a little nuts. I'd get so tense! When I couldn't stand it anymore, I'd run out to my car, blast the music loud as hell, and speed down country roads as fast as I could, windows down, music blaring, tires screaming, me rocking wildly back and forth. That movement gave me some release. It was sort of a cheap high. It was kind of crazy. It was dangerous! I thought it was about going nowhere fast, but going always takes you somewhere."

Remembering these words that Gordon had shared reminded me of how much I missed him and his stories. I pulled out my cell phone and called the hospital. The doctor told me that Gordon was still alive but barely!

"He's in a deep sleep and very fragile," he stressed. "Surprisingly, his blood pressure has stabilized since we last talked, and I am cautiously hopeful.

"It may take as long as twenty-four to thirty-six hours to bring him out of the coma once the waking process begins. I'll call if there are any changes."

Cautiously hopeful sounded like good news to me! I was behind schedule and was glad for the extra travel time.

UNEXPECTED PASSENGER

Gradually, I reached the posted speed limit as the wind blew my road map off the passenger seat and into the back of the car. It seemed deliberate, as if someone tossed it out of the way to make room.

"Make yourself comfortable, Gordon. We've got miles to go," I said out loud to no one at all.

My conversation with Mom at her barbecue made up most of the words I'd spoken since leaving home. I needed a travel companion, and Gordon seemed available!

It felt appropriate to imagine Gordon into the car along with what he might say.

"I'm tired of talking to myself, Gordon. Share some of your erudite observations!"

"Looks like Texas," he mumbled, "so I thought I'd ride along. I would have preferred joining you somewhere in Europe! I do have my passport!

"Yes, I know you have all the legal documents for travel abroad, but—"

"Speak up! You sound like you're a million miles away."

"Is this better?" I belted out as I wiped the sweat from my forehead.

"It's better, but I think it would be cooler in Switzerland!"

"I'm sure, but—"

"I was born here," Gordon interrupted, pointing out at the landscape we were traversing. "I was born somewhere out there in the miles and miles of the same hot, dry, baked shit.

"There were times when I thought I'd never get out.

"Sony wanted to be buried in a shallow canyon out there someplace. You didn't bury her ashes there, did you?"

"No. I couldn't do it. It was too lonely a place. She showed me the exact spot when I flew out here to help her and your mother with selling your boyhood house and its contents.

"We had days of yard sales in the scorching heat. Very few people showed up, but one guy that knew your father purchased a really fine collection of drafting tools. They were in a locking leather-covered box and looked as if they'd never been used."

"I remember those! How much did you sell them for?"

"Two hundred dollars! It was the most expensive thing on the table."

"And worth every penny!"

"I sold your old train set and some games but saved the Ben-Hur chariot figures for my kids."

"I reenacted that chariot-race scene a thousand times after seeing the movie. Sony took me to see it in 1959. I begged her to hide in the theater so we could watch it again, and she said yes. We ducked down and hid between showings, pretending we were hiding from the Romans. I remember liking the idea that she said yes even more than I liked the movie. Sony was always there for me. She'd make a big deal about anything I drew or wrote or did.

"The night before Sony left to go to college, she fell asleep while reading a story to me in my bedroom. Every time she'd finish one, I'd ask for another and then another until sleep kept her in my room all night. That's where I always wanted her.

"I was surprised that Sony took our mother back east to live with her. They never got along."

"You know, Gordon, in the end, they did! Things changed once your mother got help. The big turning point came back in eighty-five, when Sony asked your mother to join the travel group I was taking to Paris and London."

"Why did you do that trip? Whatever prompted you to take thirteen people to Europe for ten days? Most of them didn't even know each other."

"I knew them all. I also knew that most of them might never do it on their own and thought it would be fun to share something I loved so much. We had a ball. We had our surprises and challenges, but when it was all over with, they had each gone beyond their expectations, and Sony and your mother were friends."

"You know, you're a born teacher, don't you?

"No, Gordon, I'm a born student."

"Along with being an asshole!" He kidded. "I wish I could have gone on that trip with you."

"We sent you postcards."

"Not the same."

"No."

BARRACUDA

We were silent for a long time, and I thought about Gordon's sister who had flown back to Philadelphia with her mother after the homestead had been sold.

Sony was beginning to show early signs of potential health issues, and I feared Wilma would be more than she could handle.

I watched Sony, periodically, fumble for words, have moments of confusion, and lose items that she'd just had in her hand.

I wouldn't let myself think it was anything more than forgetfulness under the stress of the move. The symptoms weren't always present, and I convinced myself that it was all in my imagination.

It wasn't!

"Matthew, my middle son, flew to Texas with me to lend a hand packing up your mother's house. He turned sixteen and was going to help drive the rented truck with the household goods and clothes across country. For Matt, it was a great adventure, and I loved having that special time with him. Matt also loved driving your 1965 Plymouth Barracuda that was left in the garage when you went into the Navy. It was a classic ride and still desired by youthful dragsters. A neighbor bought it."

"That car was my girl. How I could make her dance!"

"Matthew talked about that Barracuda halfway to New Orleans."

"You should have bought it for him."

"I couldn't afford it. That neighbor paid top dollar, and your mother needed that money."

"She should have given it to you for all the work you did."

"I did the work because I wanted to. No payment was needed!"

"There's a sucker born every minute!"

We watched the tumbleweeds rolling across the highway and into the distance. Then without changing his gaze on the horizon, he asked, "Where did you bury Sony's ashes?

"In our garden next to your mother's! They're near a yellow rose bush and a little pond."

"Is that where I'll be going?"

"No! There's a restroom in a local porn shop with peep-shows and a toilet that hasn't seen a scrub brush in thirty years. I thought I'd flush you there."

"Well, learn this, asshole, I better be in that fucking garden!"

"Wouldn't you rather be in the garden fucking?"

"In my dreams, brother! In my dreams!"

INTUITION

"Tell me. When you and Matthew went to New Orleans, was that your first visit to the city of Mardi Gras madness?"

"No, I'd been there with a college friend Otis during my junior year. It was an impromptu road trip from Kansas over the Thanksgiving break. My older sister had sent me five dollars, and I already had twenty bucks in my wallet. With that plus what Otis contributed, we figured that if we slept in the car and only ate the cereal we'd scrounged from the school's cafeteria, we could make it.

"Somewhere near Beaumont, Texas, we pulled off the highway to sleep. We'd seen a lot of cops on the highway and thought it would be best to find a nice quiet suburban neighborhood to park the car for the night. I found a spot without a streetlight to keep us up and pulled in next to the curb. I grabbed my sleeping bag and jumped into the back seat while Otis stretched out in the front.

"He was snoring within seconds, but I was stirred by thoughts that we were not where we were supposed to be. After a few minutes, I woke him up, saying I had to move the car as I pushed myself behind the wheel."

"Why?" he groaned. "Is something wrong?"

"It's just a feeling," I answered while putting the car in reverse and backing up one car length in anticipation of going around the block to find another spot. But as soon as

I finished backing up, that feeling I'd had disappeared, and I turned off the engine.

"What now?" Otis asked.

"It's okay now! This feels better," I said while returning to my sleeping bag and closing my eyes.

"Page, you're a little crazy! You know that, don't you?"

"Go to sleep, Otis," I said and he did.

At four thirty in the morning, we were shaken awake by a tremendous scraping noise and loud crash! While we slept, another car had parked in the space we had vacated, and a third car had sideswiped ours and demolished the car in front of us.

I could see that the driver of the car who'd struck us wasn't even moving.

"He's drunk," I heard somebody yell. "Look at all those beer bottles!"

He was passed out behind the wheel of his car, unaware of the neighbors turning on their lights and running out of their front door.

I slowly backed up into a driveway and then pulled out in the direction of the highway.

"I'll never question your intuitions again," Otis said as we drove into the rising sun.

"Holy crap! Do you get those feelings often?" Gordon questioned in amazement.

"All the time and all my life!"

"Do you always pay attention?"

"I learned to! My mother called it getting a heads-up. It's my norm."

"I think you're frigging weird, and I'm sure your buddy, Otis, thought so too," Gordon blurted out! "I'd call it needing your head examined!"

"If you think that's weird, just listen to this!"

"Go ahead and tell your story. I'm bored with Texas. The next time you conjure me up, it better be in Paris or Florence, Italy. I'm going to shut my eyes. You just talk. Fill my head with someplace else."

"I'll be surprised if you can't pay attention to this one."

DRINKING JAG

"During the summer of 1975, Sony went to California to attend a two-week screenwriter's class."

"Yes, I remember," Gordon said. "She stayed with me and commuted to the school. After that, she went to stay with our mother for two weeks."

"I was stopping by her apartment while she was gone to feed the cats and water the plants. One day when I was there, the phone rang, and it was Sony."

"And you're going to tell me that this coincidence was another one of your mystical intuitive revelations?"

"Don't interrupt. If you want me to transport you out of Texas, you have to keep your mouth shut!"

"Beam me up, Scotty!"

"Anyway, Sony was an absolute mess on the phone. She was crying so hard, I could hardly understand a word she was saying."

"That doesn't sound like my sister."

"It took a while for me to calm her down, and even then, she had moments when she'd burst into tears."

"What the hell was going on?"

"Your mother was on a drinking jag and was in the worst shape Sony had ever seen. Apparently, the situation had been going on since before Sony arrived. The house was a mess— no laundry had been done, no food was in the kitchen, and no bills had been paid. There were empty bottles of liquor everywhere! Your mother was exhausted and kept demanding that Sony go to the liquor store and restock the bar.

"Sony said your mother had been in her housecoat for days, and every minute was a nightmare filled with screaming words of hate, accusations, and insults."

"I know that mother!"

"Sony was supposed to fly back east in order to return to her teaching job in ten days but didn't know if she should stay and try to make things right in Texas. Of course, this would mean sacrificing her career and the life she'd worked so hard to build in Pennsylvania."

"What'd you tell her?"

"I told her to take charge and not to let the sick one have the power to make decisions. I told her to remember the strength of the strongest character she ever played on stage and adopt that personality. Then I dictated a script for the role of a lifetime, and she wrote it down."

"A script?"

"Well, maybe more like director's notes! It went like this:

"Take the keys to any vehicle! [Mail them back from Pennsylvania.]

"Throw out all medications!

"Get rid of any matches or lighters!

"Remove every knife and anything that can be used as a weapon from the house!

"Throw every liquor bottle and any reminder of the situation into the trash!

"Don't even listen to your mother. She's ill and doesn't know what's she's saying!

"Don't allow yourself to be the victim of her illness!

"Don't accept blame for anything! If you must speak, just keep repeating I love you!

"Pull the sheets off each bed, gather every piece of dirty laundry, and wash it all.

"If she tries to stop you, drag the hose in from the yard, turn it on full blast, and chase her into her bedroom. [It's summer in Texas. It will dry. She's exhausted and drunk and will sleep.]

"Clean every room!

"Organize the bills and paperwork into categories and put them into a safe spot.

"Call the local grocery store and make arrangements for a food delivery! [Enough to last two weeks!]

"Call her doctor. Explain what's been happening and make arrangements for an emergency home visit!

"As soon as the doctor leaves, pick up the phone and make a reservation to fly to New Orleans. When those arrangements are confirmed, call me. I will meet you there in two days. We'll talk! We'll have an adventure and then I'll drive you home to Pennsylvania in time for school."

"Did Sony pull it off?" Gordon questioned.

"Flawlessly!"

"And did you meet Sony in New Orleans?

"I did. I got a cheap hotel near the airport. We stayed up the entire first night talking and then decided to put the nightmare behind us and focus on the present. I called around, looking for a nicer place near where the action was. As luck would have it, I got a fantastic room in the Cornstalk Hotel. It was filled with southern charm, which helped Sony to distance herself from the Texas experience.

"We took a paddle-wheel-steamboat tour on the Mississippi right after breakfast. It was like being on the set of the 1951 musical, *Showboat*! I could almost imagine William Warfield singing 'Ol' Man River' on the deck of that boat. At the time, I never would have dreamed that I'd direct him in a musical I would write twenty years later.

"Then we did the traditional walking tour that included the French Quarter, the garden district and mansions, the Saint Louis Cemetery, Jackson Square, and Pat O'Brien's where we drank one of their famous hurricanes.

"We settled into a great spicy-shrimp meal, just as the sun was setting and then wandered down Bourbon Street as the city lights transformed everything into a Cajun carnival that emphasized the outrageous, hilarious, and sexiest stuff the city had to offer.

"Just as we were about to return to the hotel, Sony spotted a sign down a side street that read, "Palms read. Five dollars." As a lark, we decided to go in, but first, we took off everything that would have visually clued in anyone to our past. I put my school ring in my pocket, and Sony put her grandmother's beads in her purse. We both pulled out five-dollar bills before entering so that no pocketbook or wallet would be seen and reveal any details of our lives.

"We were met by an older woman who looked and sounded of Eastern Indian descent. She wore huge hoop earrings, a black loose-fitting blouse, long flowing red skirt, and purple headscarf. Every finger had a ring and a jade, scorpion necklace hung from a long gold chain.

"We said nothing as we placed the money in the palm of her open hand, each choosing one of the three stools that surrounded a small worn oak table lit by a single candle."

"Welcome! The women in my family have been practicing this art for over 4,500 years. Please relax and allow me to be one with you. I make only one promise and that is truth."

"She looked at both of us with keen, discerning eyes and said, 'Please remain silent until you leave this sanctuary. I will take your right hand one at a time, study it, and then tell you what I see, if I see anything at all. There will be no discussion! When I am done, I will nod my head. This is your signal to exit in silence.'"

"Then she looked at Sony saying, 'Place your right hand, palm up, in the palm of my left hand.'"

"Sony did exactly what was asked, nothing more and nothing less. As soon as skin touched skin, our host showed signs of a small shiver and then leaned in to study Sony's hand. At least two minutes passed in silence before she spoke."

"'I'm sorry,' she said, placing one of our five-dollar bills back on the table and holding one finger up to her lips to remind Sony not to speak."

"I can only confirm that you are a writer and that your words are and will be appreciated, but as to your future, I cannot speak!"

"Then she signaled for my hand, which brought about the same shiver and silent stare."

"I see a definite, distinct, deep, and natural cut across many of your most telling lines, but this cut does not bring an end to the others, just a pause. This is new to me, but my grandmother taught me how to read this."

"She looked into my eyes and said without blinking, 'You will die! Then you will live again in the here and now. Hold onto this rare lesson that is being offered you. Learn well and share.'

"'You are an artist! I see you also write, but your best work will not be published by signing the work as you have done. Consider another way of making your mark. One more thing,' she said as she let go of my hand, picked up a pencil, and began writing what appeared to be a scrambled alphabet on a crinkled piece of paper. She suddenly stopped, looked at me, and without looking down, began to circle different letters. Then she copied those letters in a particular order at the bottom of the paper, turned it around, and pushed it to me. It read, 'Cleora Virginia Cooper.' She put her finger to her lips again, took back the paper, and set it on fire with the flame from the candle on the table. We left as the blue smoke from the crumbling ash curled in the air and disappeared."

"What was written on that paper?"

"I was so stunned. I could hardly speak but answered, 'My mother's maiden name!'"

"You're making this up!" Gordon blurted out. "All this witch did was identify the sucker in you and take your money."

"Perhaps, but in fact, Sony had no future to be read, and I did die but lived. Some things cannot be explained."

"If you can't explain it, what do you do with it?"

"Accept it!"

"How does the data-driven, logical, scientifically based side of you do that?"

"I have a glass of red wine with the intuitive, artistic, and creative other half and dream."

"Well, David, I think you're nuts, but it was a good story anyway. I think you ought to make time to write this shit down."

"I will when I can figure out what all these stories mean. Meanwhile, I'll just keep collecting them."

"Meanwhile, do you have another one?"

LIFE IN HELL

"I'm doing the driving, Gordon. You tell me a story."

"Boring! Oh, so boring!"

"Let me be the judge of that. Come on, you slacker. Do your best to keep me awake for the next hundred miles. You owe me. You're way behind in telling your share!"

"Just remember, you made me do this. Where in hell do I start? Never mind. I'll just rearrange those words a little. My life started in hell!"

"Oh! For God's sake, Gordon! I didn't like this story the first time you told it. I'm not going to like it any better now!"

"You asked for it, and now you're going to get it. My life started in hell, but at first, I didn't recognize it. I know it well now 'cause I've had to revisit different sections of the abyss so often. At first, it was just confusion. I was loved, I think. There were birthday parties and presents under the Christmas tree and books on the shelves.

"There was food on the table and clean clothes in the drawer. All that was in place, like a perfect, well-thought-out stage set! I went to school. I participated in activities, and to the outside world, I was an average kid in an average house on a dirt road south of San Antonio.

"My mother dabbled with paints, kept a clean house, cooked reasonably good food, and made the appropriate fuss when I did the right thing or the wrong thing. She often walked around the inside of the house, going from room to room, looking with despair out each window. Her pacing reminded me of a tiger I once saw at the zoo. First, this way and then that way, again and again, like a caged animal trapped and going slowly mad.

"My father was a civil engineer responsible for building dams and other large projects in the area. He was mathematical and structured. His schedule was unbreakable and pencils always sharp. He liked things organized, his meals on time, and no bumps in the road. He always left his newspaper folded and ashtray without an ash. The car was washed and waxed every Saturday followed by a long nap that was always interrupted by my mother, begging to go out somewhere and do something. I couldn't stand the begging. At times, I hated them both.

"Eventually, my father seemed to never fully awaken from the naps that got longer and longer. Even when he did, he wasn't himself. He started to be late for work, then he would get lost on his way to work, and finally, he didn't know what work was. By that time, my mother was having an affair with my father's boss. I got to witness the entire fucking mess while trying to distract myself with television shows like *Father Knows Best*, and *Leave It to Beaver* where there was always a happy ending, and the mother never drank whiskey from a bottle hidden in the pantry behind a box of cornflakes."

"I'm pulling over. I've got to puke."

I did pull over. I don't even know why. Perhaps because the memory of when Gordon first told me that story made me want to throw up.

As a kid, I had to learn how to support a mother I loved. Gordon had to learn to tolerate a mother he didn't even like.

I could feel the pain that Gordon had buried, like an ulcer left untreated for decades.

I got out of the car, took deep breaths, and slowly got my stomach settled down.

PARADISE

When I did get back behind the wheel, I wasn't sure whether Gordon would still be there, but several miles down the road, I heard, "Your turn! Tell me more about little Davey and growing up in paradise."

"It wasn't all a fairytale!"

"Prove it! Tell the story, and there better be some shit in it. Try not to make it a musical comedy. I don't want to have to kill you on this sunny Texas day. If there's any dancing, I'll grab the wheel and head for the nearest cliff. We can be the male version of Thelma and Louise."

"Do that, and you'll be going over with me!"

"Nope! I'm not really here, remember? Let your story take me to Syracuse and try to keep me interested."

"My parents moved to Syracuse, New York, and started a family. There were three of us kids. I was the middle child and only boy!"

"I know all that. Get to the shit part. I want drunken name-calling pot-throwing arguments that ended in tears and booze. Give me something I can identify with!"

"We were taught to dance in our tiny kitchen where I waxed the linoleum floor, making it good for quick turns."

"You bastard," Gordon screamed and then we laughed. I laughed so hard, I could hardly drive. The contrast of our two worlds was a collision so great that we either had to sob or laugh like hell. We both chose to laugh, which made me think we might not be so different after all.

"Is Ginger Rogers in this?"

"No, and neither is Fred Astaire. Now shut up! My mother was our dance instructor as well as everything else. My father wasn't there for the dance lessons. He was busy—"

"Fucking your first-grade teacher?" Gordon interrupted.

"He was busy working, trying to keep us in post-World War II suburbia, you asshole!

"While he worked, I became his miniature stand in, held hostage by grown-up things, watching over my baby sister, comforting my mother, earning the label of being the good boy for the price of my youth."

"Sounds a little shitty, like a wet fart but no big mess!"

"Do you want to hear this or not?"

"Go ahead! I'll try not to doze."

"Thousands of men came home from the war looking for jobs that just weren't there. In the Army, my father had been a supply sergeant and war hero, receiving multiple medals, including the Silver Star and Purple Heart.

"The Silver Star was earned by volunteering to be part of a small group whose mission it was to sneak into enemy territory and rescue an officer who'd been captured. They were successful! When I was a kid, I must have heard that story a thousand times. I always wanted my father to rescue me."

"Rescue you from what? Disneyland? Now I want to puke! Anything too sweet upsets my stomach."

"Quiet! It's my story. Let me tell it. None of the medals helped him to get work on the home front. After a short stint delivering coal, he got a job driving a city bus. It might not have been the job he wanted, but he made the best of it. He worked as many shifts and hours of overtime that they would give him.

"My father used to say he felt lucky to have any job at all. He said lots of guys never came home from the war, or they came home in pieces.

"I remember men with no legs, wearing tattered remains of old uniforms, propped up on carts along Salina Street, selling pencils. My father never passed them without putting money in their tin cup. He never took a pencil."

"Of course not! Did he also walk on water?"

I continued speaking but louder, "Being the only boy, I got three times the dance practice as my sisters! I was the obvious partner for everyone. At night, if my mother felt well enough, there would be an extra dance lesson. I didn't mind. It gave me something to do besides playing with my race car set or drawing. It was better than sitting at the kitchen window, watching it snow.

"During the long upstate New York winters, all us guys in the neighborhood would race each other home after school. We'd use the limited daylight hours to build forts and wage war with snowballs and the occasional icicle. The wars often ended with some hand-to-hand combat. I attributed my ability to win the wrestling matches to the quick turns and recovery tactics I'd learned in the kitchen.

"My father rarely got to see my victories. He was usually working, and when the snow fell, his workdays were longer. Maybe that helped me too. Since he wasn't around, I heaped the coal into the furnace and carried the heavy ash barrel up from the basement.

"I also shoveled mountains of snow. I did lots of things that made me stronger than most other kids my age. Even in the summer, my father had little time to play catch or go camping or anything. If I questioned him, he'd say, 'Duty first!'

"That was the First Division's motto. He said those words were what got him through Europe. I didn't even know what Europe was.

"When there was a little time for my father and me to be together, he would talk about the war. I knew all the names of his closest buddies from the First Division by heart: Dinatto, Farina, Orient, Kelly, Patterson, and Rizzo. When he talked about them, he became animated and alive with emotion and energy. I felt like he wasn't even with me at all.

"The movie in his head was punctuated with bomb blasts accented with the piercing sound of incoming missiles. He was in Africa or Europe, still fighting the war. When he wasn't at work, or sleeping, he was at the American Legion where the kind of stories my father told were at the center of every conversation. Even in my father's uneasy sleep, he yelled out and would break into a sweat as if the war raged on inside him.

"I suppose his duty really was to earn the money to pay the mortgage, put food on the table, and everything! I appreciated what he did for all of us. But his duty made me worry about money all the time. I told this to my mother, and she said that my duty was to be a good boy! I tried. I did what I was told. I obeyed the rules. I kept my room clean. I thought that if I did my duty, bad things couldn't happen. I was wrong."

"What could go wrong? Nobody was drunk? Your mother didn't introduce you to another long-lost Uncle Frank or Uncle George or Uncle Whatever before going out to God knows where!"

"When I was a kid, I never knew what the truth was. At least you had facts to deal with. I had to juggle lies, doubts, and innuendoes. You can't argue with sincerity! I had to guess what was real every day. You can't fully invest in what or who you don't trust, and when you can't figure it out, you learn to never trust anyone, never commit to anyone, never love anyone!"

"I thought you were too tired to talk!"

"I'm exhausted! I'm weary. I'm sorry I interrupted. I just get angry sometimes. I'll keep my mouth shut while you tell your story."

"I'm not sure I want to anymore."

"You want to keep me here, don't you?"

"I do, but my story is important to me. It's all I have to share. I don't tell it to make you feel lousy or angry or bad. I tell it, seeking to find the building blocks of my own life. I want to know what has made me who I am."

"I apologize! I'll sift through the rubble with you.

"Pick it up from where you left off. I want to be here. I may not be able to identify with the characters, but I like the results the story line produced.

"I do feel a bit woozy and pulled in multiple directions, but the sound of your voice is the anchor I need to keep me here while I figure out my own life.

"How did your mother teach you to dance?"

DANCING ETIQUETTE 101

"My sisters and my mother all danced differently. I was taught to adjust my maneuverings to meet the needs of each partner. 'Take the lead,' my mother would say. 'But remember it's your job to make the girl look her best. The dance isn't about the man,' she explained. 'It's about the woman.' She taught me how to stand, 'posture is everything,' and how to keep my chin up, 'be proud,' and how to lead with that first all-important step. 'Take command. Be confident. Be strong!' Most importantly, she showed me exactly where to put the palm of my right hand in the small of my partner's back. 'Do this correctly, and a woman will follow you anywhere,' she'd say. She was right!

"I won my first dance contest in sixth grade! The prize was a top-forty vinyl recording of 'Duke of Earl.' It was presented to me by my elementary principal in the school cafeteria where the sock hop was held. I didn't think it was such a big deal, but by seventh grade, I began to appreciate dancing with any girl that wasn't my mother or my sister.

"In eighth grade, classmates used to form a circle around me and whoever I was dancing with. There would be shouts and applause as we'd twist or do the Mashed Potato, or the Jerk, all popular dances I learned on the fly without my mother. Dick Clark's *American Bandstand* was a tremendous help in teaching me how young people were dancing. The black-and-white television in our living room opened my eyes up to moves that weren't going to be taught in the kitchen. That TV also brought old movies into my world and gave me a chance to watch how men led their partners in films like *Silk Stockings*, *American in Paris*, and *Singing in the Rain*. It also brought me the old war movies and a glimpse of that military partner my father still danced with.

"I learned to square dance in gym class and even joined the school's folk dance club. Once, I got to dance on the Jim Deline show, a local TV program that everybody watched.

"I was known as the kid who could dance. It came easy to me. The hard part was defending my masculinity from those who misinterpreted my ability to move to the music. They gave me many opportunities to make adjustments to their point of view, and I had the raw knuckles to prove it.

"Other things did not come as easy to me as dancing. There were gaps in my core knowledge in direct relation to the absence of my father. At times, I could be very shy, but on the dance floor, I was king. I never had to ask anyone to dance. They asked me. They lined up to ask me! The dance floor was my world, and I could control every corner of it. It might not have given me the same social prestige as being on the football team, but it didn't hurt, especially when it came to girls, and I was beginning to find girls more and more interesting all the time!

"After watching the Olympics on television, I became fascinated with gymnastics. I'd linger for a few minutes after school watching the gym teacher instruct the team, learning the moves needed for a winning routine in floor exercise.

"I'd practice the moves over and over in my backyard until they came as natural as breathing. By the time I was in ninth grade, I'd learned to incorporate handsprings and splits into some of my more athletic dances. I wanted to join the gymnastics team, but someone had to be at home for my little sister. There was no way out of the lawn that needed mowing, hedge to clip, garden to weed, and other chores that waited for me.

"My older sister had discovered her own way to deal with everything. She seemed to lose herself in books and in an air of sophistication that made household tasks beneath her. Don't misunderstand. She also had her duty list, the piano to polish, furniture to dust, and dishes to wash, but it ended there. I didn't hate her for it. She had been the one I used to call Sissy back in the days before my little sister came along, back before my mother was sick, back when Sissy would read to me and tell me everything would be all right.

"I wanted to find a way *out* and looked for it every day. I wanted to be listened to, heard, known, saved, but at least I had dance and that was better than nothing. Even with the addition of flips into my routine, I'd remember to end every dance by twirling my partner fast and furiously, leaving her and the onlookers dizzy and wanting more. The dizziness became my temporary *out*, and I was grateful for it."

THE KID WHO COULD DANCE

"In tenth grade, I left the security of my neighborhood junior high and took the bus to North Syracuse Central High School. It was a big place where thousands of kids from different junior highs came to complete their last three years of public education. I felt invisible and lost in the crowded hallways. I got turned around ten times the first day. I was even late to homeroom, arriving just as they announced that school dances would be held on the first Friday of every month.

"This announcement gave me some hope of regaining my identity until I arrived at the dance along with hundreds of other tenth, eleventh, and twelfth graders. I couldn't find anybody I knew. The music was playing, but for the first time, I wasn't dancing. I wasn't being watched. I was watching. That's when I saw her. I saw this girl who moved just like the kids I'd seen on television. She was freed by the music, transformed into something wild, and I wanted to dance with her.

"I watched her dance again and again with the same guy who couldn't dance at all. He was stiff and awkward, unable to showcase her talent. The guy looked a bit older and was hanging with a group of seniors who went outside to smoke about every third dance.

"I asked someone I finally recognized from class if he knew that girl in the short black skirt and white top. The only thing he said was 'That's Linda. Don't go there! That guy she's with will knock your teeth out!'

"During one of his smoke breaks, I watched that girl impatiently waiting while a great set of tunes played. She kept looking back toward the doors, but he wasn't coming. I don't know what came over me, but I found myself moving through the crowd of dancers, avoiding hips and flying elbows until I was by her side.

"'Want to dance?' I asked, surprising myself. She took one final glace at the doors and then stepped toward me just as "Downtown" by Petula Clark boomed from the DJ's speakers.

"She started to do the shimmy, a dance which fit the upbeat tempo but was more suited for a real rock-and-roll song. 'How about trying this,' I said as I held her in a more traditional stance and led her through the crowd with a couple of quick spins. She responded to my every cue.

"With a little pressure from the heel of my right hand, I could direct her anywhere on the dance floor. With a raise of my left hand, I could signal turns. If I pushed her away, she'd go with the momentum as we both spun in opposite directions and returned on the beat, ready for the next move. I taught her how to break open a closed position to let me swing her over my back. As she released in a twirl, I'd catch her hand and pull her into a quick series of death-defying spins. A crowd formed around us. It was magic! We danced until they turned off the music and turned up the lights. By that time, I was that kid who could dance again!

"After I'd kissed her good night, I walked across the school yard and stood on the shoulder of Route 11, trying to hitch a ride home. My parents didn't like me hitchhiking, but

I didn't worry about it. I never looked like someone to mess with and rarely was. The streets emptied out quickly, and I began to think I'd be walking all the way home."

A DIFFERENT PARTNER

"A jacked-up dark-blue Chevy slowed down but never stopped. I walked about a quarter of a mile before taking the shortcut through the unlit parking lot behind Sweetheart Market. That's when I saw that blue Chevy again. The driver gunned the engine, circled me twice in tight turns, tires squealing on the payment, stones flying. He screeched to a stop with the car facing my direction and got out, engine still running. I was blinded by the headlights, but I didn't need to see who it was to know who it was.

"He walked toward me in silhouette, rolling up his sleeves, saying, 'Dancing boy!'

"'Are you sure you want to do this?' I asked, pulling off my jacket and letting it fall to the ground. 'One of us is going to get hurt, and it's not going to be me.'

"He charged at me in an all-out run, attempting a full-body tackle. I threw my hips to the left, faked the move, and then dodged to the right. He bought the fake, tripped on the toe of my trailing shoe, and fell with all his weight onto his right side. Recovering and angered by the deception, he stood, faced me, and tried again. At the last second, I turned my back on him, ducked my head, and fell into a low crouch with one leg stretched out behind me and my finger-tips touching the pavement for balance. He fell over me in a face-plant onto the loose stones. His recovery was slower this time, and when he stood, he had a face full of blood."

"'You can move, asshole, but can you stand and fight?' he yelled, wiping blood from his forehead.

"I stood my ground and raised my fists, saying, 'Let's see,' wondering if I could play by his rules. I'd learned early on that if a guy was going to dance, he'd better be prepared to fight. I had to prove this again and again since I was twelve. This joker was big, and I could see the scuffle was going to be on his terms.

"I took his first punch to the face and next one to my stomach, which knocked me back about three feet and forced all the air out of my lungs. The sound of his fist crunching against my face was worse than the pain. I felt red hot all over and a little disoriented in the dark.

"'How'd you like that?' he shouted as I brought my fists up and we circled each other. 'I'm going to teach you a brand-new dance. It's called the stomp!'

"'I didn't figure you as a talker,' I said, feeling my right eye begin to swell.

"His next two jabs caught me under my chin, snapping my head back, temporality knocking me off-balance. Then he slammed me with a crosscut, splitting my upper lip. While I teetered on one foot, he connected another blow to my stomach.

"I dropped back about five feet, trying to shake off the nausea and gain some time.

"'Thanks for the lesson,' I said, spitting out a mouthful of blood as I stepped back into the game. 'You might be sorry. I'm a quick learner.'

"I hit him with my next punch and the next and the next, each one connecting with his upper body. Now that I had seen his moves, I knew what to expect. I saw how he led with his right fist, dropping his left shoulder, telegraphing his every step. He also neglected to shift his weight back and forth and left his torso unprotected after bigger swings. The longer we fought, the more I could anticipate what was coming. I'd paid a price for this lesson, but it was worth it.

"I baited him by dropping my left fist and forearm. I'd been using this to protect my face from his uppercuts. He thought I was unguarded and took a swing, which I deflected with my right arm. There he was, completely vulnerable, and he knew it. I saw it in his eyes right before I landed a powerful hook to the right side of his head with my left fist. His whole body spun and collapsed in a loose tumble in front of his car lights.

"Exhausted, I leaned against the car's grill and then slid down to the ground where he was rolling over to see what would happen next.

"'Are we done here?' I asked, out of breath and bleeding.

"'Yeah,' he said. 'We're done.'

"'Can you give me a ride home?' I asked.

"'Yeah,' he said, shaking his head.

"I stood, extended my hand, and pulled him to his feet.

"It's funny how it is with guys. Once a few punches are thrown, it's over. I think we could have gone out for a couple of beers had we been old enough to be served. It was a quiet ride as we drove toward the city. I could see a steady stream of headlights on Route 81 and wondered what it would be like to be in one of those cars. It's hard to be old enough to want to go and too young to make it happen.

"I tried running away once. I had my reasons. My mother was sick. The sicker she got, the more it seemed like Syracuse was quicksand, sucking me down. I felt claustrophobic, smothered by all the things that were expected of me. One night, I gathered some stuff together and stood with my thumb out along Route 81. First, I tried going north, then south and then north again. The direction really didn't matter. No one stopped! Around three in the morning, I walked back home, determined to find some life of my own no matter where I had to look for it.

"'So,' I said to my boxing partner as he dropped me off in front of my house, 'should I be on the lookout for this car on dark nights?'

"'I may not give you a lift, but we're okay,' he said, reaching up to shake my hand."

THIRSTY

Talking out loud in the Texas heat made me dehydrated. I felt like my tongue was stuck to the roof of my mouth and was as thirsty as I'd ever been.

"Don't stop there," Gordon shouted. "Your story was just getting interesting, and I'll tell you it was about fucking time! I particularly enjoyed the part where you got punched in the face!"

"I'm glad you enjoyed that! I've got to get something to drink before I die. It's got to be 110 degrees in here. I need some water."

"You need a cold beer and time in the shade. Get off at the next exit. We'll find something."

I took the next exit and found a little town with a bar advertising the best tacos in Texas. Gordon insisted we stop, and we did, though he didn't get out of the car.

"Just leave the windows open! Have a beer and a taco for me!"

I thought I wanted water until Gordon mentioned a cold beer. I walked through the cool dark space and up to the bar. A middle-aged full-bearded bartender started rattling off the names of all the beers he had on tap as he approached. His every word was heavy with an exaggerated deep Texas drawl as he exhaled an earthy aroma of weed and tobacco. After taking another draw from the fattest cigar I'd ever seen, he impatiently waited for my order.

"Give me something local if you've got it."

"Oh, thank God," he proclaimed in a fully animated voice undiminished by the room's thick smoke and background chatter.

"When I saw your Pennsylvania license plate on the car, I thought I'd be pulling a Bud Light. I've got two Mexican beers on tap that are far from light and close to heaven!"

"I'll take one of each and a couple of tacos."

"Beef or chicken?"

"Beef!"

"You're batting a thousand, buddy. If I ever do get out of Texas, maybe I'll give Pennsylvania a try. Do you want both beers at the same time?"

"Absolutely! I've been driving for hours, and I'm the thirstiest bastard in Texas."

He looks over at a table of four farmworkers talking in Spanish and calls out while pointing at me. "Mexican beer, tacos, and he swears too! The next thing you know, he'll be telling me he rides a motorcycle!"

"I do but not this trip!"

"Here's the beer. The tacos will be up in a couple of minutes. Nice to know there's at least one real man back east."

Both beers were dark amber, icy cold with a nice head of suds and were gone before the tacos arrived. The jukebox was kicking out some upbeat Mexican tunes, and suddenly, I felt way too comfortable for someone who still had miles to go.

After eating and pissing my brains out, I walked around the unpaved parking lot, trying to recommit to the road. Finally, I got back in the car and found my way to the highway only to pull into the next rest stop and park in the shade of the only tree I'd seen in the last fifty miles.

"Time for a nap, Gordon," I said to the empty seat next to me as the sweat trickled down my face. I slept, inspiring a memory that spawned a dream.

NOT EVERYBODY CAN TAKE IT

When Sony and I took Gordon to Baltimore to visit the Inner Harbor years ago, it was a hot and humid day without shade, and I was worried about him getting overheated. Our goal was to get to the end of the pier, which jutted way out into the water, providing a great view of the city and the bay. I suggested we eat first to give Gordon a chance to rest in some air-conditioning. We found a spectacular place, which always delighted Gordon who looked forward to meals in restaurants and conversations around the table. Eating at a restaurant created an equal playing field for Gordon. We all sat at the same level, sharing eye contact and food. He'd always dock his chair as close to the table as possible, hiding his wheels under the tablecloth.

Most of his meals at home were delivered by strangers and eaten alone and in silence. This was an authentic Italian dining experience, with white linen napkins, fine wine and a waiter who looked like Pavarotti. Gordon said he expected the waiter to perform an aria every time he approached the table. We lingered long after the wine was gone and dessert eaten, talking and laughing and remembering multiple different outings, before asking for the bill.

Halfway down the pier, I was dripping with sweat and thought we should turn back, but Gordon had seen a ship similar to the one on which he'd been a gunner's mate, and he wanted to get a closer look. We strolled far out on the pier, watching storm clouds building in the east as he talked about the Navy and how he'd exercise on the deck of the ship in scorching heat while out at sea. "I'd run the length of the ship over and over, looking out at the never-ending water, thinking I traded the vast desert of the southwest for a giant frying pan! Same sun, different location."

On our way to the end of the pier, we passed another wheelchair-bound man about half of Gordon's age who was approaching from the opposite direction. "Afghanistan, I'll bet," Gordon whispered. Gordon stopped and turned his chair around for a better look, and I stopped with him. The chair this man was strapped into was similar to Gordon's battery-powered model, and the passing had been without acknowledgement from either party. There was a shared moment of electronic whir and that was it.

The other man came to a stop as well and turned his chair to look out over the water. Then without anything but the electronic whir, he pushed the red lever forward and drove his chair off the pier. The chair with its contents went straight to the bottom. Gordon sat in silence as surrounding tourists screamed and ran to the edge of the pier. Then we heard the pounding of footsteps from running policemen followed by sirens and emergency boats and divers. Gordon started his chair again, and we went past the spot where a concentration of bubbles was still breaking the water's surface.

"Free at last!" he said as the bubbles burst into thin air. Then he looked at me and added, "Not everybody can take it." Gordon took the lead—faster than Sony and I could walk—back to the van and shade.

Everyone slept as I drove what we called the tour bus back to Pennsylvania. Gordon was leaving the next day, and

I was sorry our adventure had to end in such a tragic way. I tried not to think about the young disabled man on the ocean's floor and remembered another pier I'd been on years earlier under different circumstances.

ZEUS

Sony had joined my son, Michael, and me in Athens, Greece, when he was a teenager. Our goal was to fly to Crete and then motorcycle across the island, stopping at all the historic sites along the way. Michael was extremely happy to have this trip happen because it had been postponed for a year because of my stroke. He and my doctors didn't think anything like this would ever be in my future, but I was determined to prove them wrong. Not all things worked perfectly, but being an actor, I knew how to fake it.

I'd made arrangements for us to stay on a farm outside Heraklion where they grew grapes. They also raised goats, and chickens. It came with authentic Greek food and a private beach. It was near to the port where twice a week at three in the morning, you could catch a boat to Patras on the Greek mainland.

For three days, we toured the White Mountains and swam in crystal-clear azure waters. It was heaven! Michael took particular interest in Mount Ida, the tallest mountain in the range and home to the Ideon Cave, which, according to Greek mythology, is where Zeus was born. We all had too much sun, too much ouzo, and too much traditional Greek food! It was great, but all too soon, it was time to catch that boat back.

We stuffed everything into our backpacks and walked away from the soft yellow lights of the farm into the dark of the sandy shoreline as we made our way to the pier. One single low-watt bulb hung, dangling in the breeze from a wire attached to a rusting flagpole where the sand met the pier.

We were told to hang the red banner we'd been given as far up on that pole as possible. They said the boat's searchlights would scan the shoreline for the signal that passengers were waiting at the end of the pier.

As we walked down the pier, away from the shore into total blackness, it felt as if we were walking on the water itself. The sky was strewn with stars, and the surface of the water reflected them perfectly, disorienting me with the sensation that I was in the sky.

We all laid down on the pier using our backpacks as pillows, staring into the heavens and allowed Zeus, the god of sky, lightning, and thunder to carry us away. No one spoke. The experience was too perfect for words. An hour passed, and suddenly, the spell was broken by the bright lights and loud horn of the approaching boat.

I will always remember being on that particular pier as one of the most perfect moments of my life.

Not so with the pier I'd been on with Gordon where I still picture those bubbles, signaling the last breath and final act of someone whose pain was too great for even Zeus to carry.

That man was weighted down by far more than a wheelchair! The ponderous load anchored his spirit and pulled his eyes shut, blinding him from the sky and all that shines within it. Only those with incredible strength can manage that burden.

From that moment on, I always thought of Gordon as the strongest person I knew.

THE ARGUMENT

After my short nap on the side of the road in the Texas heat, my invisible passenger was eager to get moving.

"You know you snore, right?"

"So?"

"So I couldn't get any rest at all with you sounding like a chainsaw in the next seat! How'd you ever get a woman to stay in bed with you?"

"By promising I wasn't interested in sleep!"

Gordon howled as I pulled back onto the highway.

"Is it my turn, or yours?"

"Turn for what?"

"To tell a story!"

"I'm positive I told the last one."

"I'm sure it's your turn. Besides, I'm doing all the driving."

"And the snoring! You owe me after what you made me suffer through!"

"Come on. Dig deep. Come up with something interesting."

"You'll be sorry. It won't have any dancing in it!"

"I've got that particular topic covered! Come on. Shock me with something original: a wild night with a dark-haired beauty in Singapore, some adventure, or tale of a love lost."

"Keep rattling off ideas. You're bound to trigger something. You're the creative type. Get a little complicated. Put more than one theme into play. I can handle it, if you can.

Try suggesting topic ideas that are more on the fringe, things that are out of the norm."

"How about a decision you made that was good and bad at the same time? I added the bad part, just to keep you interested."

"All right. I'll bite! I'm going to expound on that good-and-bad abstract concept you just suggested."

"Don't forget the good part of the story."

"Don't worry. It will be in there. Just let me collect my thoughts for a minute."

"I'm all ears, patiently waiting."

"Okay, here we go! It was a dark and stormy night—"

"Come on, Gordon!"

"No, really, it was a dark and stormy night, and I was awakened by a severe shaking that practically threw me out of my bed! At first, I thought it was an earthquake. The blankets and sheet were in a tangle and in the dim light that came in the window from the street. I could see my legs twitching and fingers moving as if I was playing the guitar.

"I was filled with overwhelming joy, believing that somehow someway, my spinal cord was miraculously healing. I couldn't control the movements, but they were happening, and absolutely nothing had moved since the accident.

"I shouted out with excitement, but there was no one there to hear me. I desperately wanted a witness to verify what I was seeing. I wanted to say, 'Look! See what's happening. I'm moving. I'm moving!' Within a few minutes, everything settled down, and I lay there thinking that the doctors were all wrong. I wanted to tell them that I was going to walk again and run again and play the guitar again and have sex again, and the next morning, after my aide found me in a knot of bedclothes, half in and half out of the bed, I convinced him to take me to the hospital to see my doctor. I told him what had happened and all the things I was going to do when I got back on my feet. I was already thinking of how I was going to donate my electric chair and access van to the Veteran's Hospital. There was also this certain girl I wanted to call!

"As we were on our way to the doctor, I was imagining going to the places you've gone. I saw myself hiking and climbing mountains and maybe even dancing.

"I had read about scientists working on new and different methods for spinal repair and hoped that one day I'd walk again. But now, this spontaneous healing meant I didn't have to wait for new procedures and government approvals. It was happening on its own, and I was going to be all right!

"The doctor was very kind and very patient and very sure that what I experienced was just a strong spasm. He showed me the x-rays of my neck and back and with great care, shared that the spasms would be getting worse and become dangerous for me."

"'They could throw you right out of your wheelchair as well as your bed,' he said. 'Now that we know you are experiencing these things, your license will be revoked. You can't drive no matter what sophisticated engineering has been installed in your van. It's the law!'

"So one minute, I was about to participate in the Olympics, and the next, I was back in the wheelchair, smacked in the face by fucking reality. I asked the doctor if there was anything that could be done to permanently stop the spasms and was told he could operate to sever the nerves that were triggering the attacks. Then he said that the operation could never be reversed and that would leave me out of the running for any future medical breakthroughs! He also said the decision was totally up to me but encouraged me to choose surgery quickly before the spasms caused additional injuries.

"I was devastated! I was speechless! I was without hope!

"I had the operation a week later. They severed the nerves, but more importantly, they severed me from my dreams."

"Gordon, I'm so sorry."

"Don't be sorry. It's just the way it is."

"You deserve better."

"Maybe, it's exactly what I deserve. I'm not a big believer in fate anyway. It seems to me that we get what we get, not what we deserve."

"Gordon, you're depressing the hell out of me. I can see the shitty decision you were faced with and the consequences resulting from that decision, but where is the good part of this story you promised?"

"The good part escaped me for a while as well, but slowly, I came to fully realize that my dreams were preventing me from conquering the obstacles that were within my reach. My dreams were so wildly unrealistic that I didn't focus on what was really possible. Dreams, like goals, need to be obtainable; otherwise, they're just fantasies. I had to do some serious self-assessment to get my head straight. Don't get me wrong. I still have a few secret dreams, but I control them instead of them controlling me. Now most of my dreams are for other people."

"I understand the need to adjust goals, but—"

"But nothing! No other point of view is needed here! My job was to tell a story, and your job was to shut up and listen. No edits or additions are accepted!"

"I'm not trying to change your mind. That story was your reality, and I have mine. I was just going keep with the same topic."

"Then make it a story, not a discussion," Gordon demanded angrily as if the sharing of the severed nerves had brought him back to a place he never wanted to visit again.

I could tell that everything Gordon had shared was packed with regret and sorrow. The operation had healed, but deep scares were still there. All these years later, there was still pain that went beyond the flesh-and-bone-deep anger!

"Is there anything I can—"

"Just tell your fucking story," he shouted impatiently. "Tell it, or shut the fuck up. I'm tired of this game."

I'd seen Gordon angry before but not like this. Whatever was driving the anger was not just me, but I was the available target!

I waited a few minutes, deciding if I wanted to tell my story or find something else that would change the subject or distract us for a while but then he spoke.

"Go ahead. Tell your story."

"Same rules?"

"Go for it! Give me your decision, the good and the bad. I can take it."

Those were his words, but there was still an edge to his voice, so I waited another minute before starting a story with similar parameters.

"Following the stroke, I did a lot of reality checks and goal adjustments. I also had to face the fact that lots of people were unable to grasp what I had experienced and expected me to be everything that I was."

"And what were you at that particular time that everyone still expected you to be?"

"I was at the top of my game! I was on a roll of successes. Lots of things were coming together for me."

"Be specific! I want to know what being on top of your game means. I've never been there. What in hell does being at the top of your game look like, feel like, taste like? I've only had the view from under the bus! Cut it up for me into digestible pieces so I can get the taste of success!" he yelled.

"Okay. I'll give you the entire meal since you've ordered it!

"I had recently directed Henry Housman's civil war play off Broadway and written, videotaped, and edited a documentary about novelist Harriet May Savitz. I'd also received a grant to record three of my short stories. Do you want more?"

"Don't leave out a single tasty morsel. Serve me what a creative genius with two good legs and working hands can accomplish, every mouthful burns, so make sure you keep it hot!"

"Gordon, this story line is of your making. You asked for this! If you can't swallow it, let's find something more palatable."

"Since it is already on the menu, I'll take a double order! Dish it out! Ladle it into me with both hands. Stuff me with your majesty. Overfill me with this culinary masterpiece of accomplishments."

"What in hell is this all about? Are you just trying to show off your vocabulary skills? What nerve have I touched?"

"You've touched them all, and they're severed, unable to respond, except in words. The table's set. Bring it on. I'm starving!"

"Then swallow this!" I yelled back, finding my own anger and letting it out.

"I was lecturing and performing all over the country. I'd just directed a successful production of my play *Recipes* and finished writing and directing a new musical, *Resisting Gravity*, starring Grammy Award-winning William Warfield. Should I continue?"

"Why not? I asked for it. Give me the entire smorgasbord of your achievements!"

"Here it comes, soup to nuts, the whole buffet!

"I was booked to perform for 1,500 people in South Carolina, and I'd written and directed a video script that was to have national distribution. I'd also completed ghostwriting a book that was going into print.

"Oh, I almost forgot. I was volunteering as a director for a production of *Romeo and Juliet* with troubled teenagers."

"Well, that would clearly put Christ on your side! Did he bring the wine?"

"Why are you being such an ass?"

"Didn't an ass carry Christ into Jerusalem? I'm just trying to be of help!"

"You can help by shutting up while I continue."

"That's enough. I can't take it anymore!"

"Oh. But you must! You asked for it, and you're going to get it.

"I had just agreed to be a consultant for a new opera, and I was participating in ASCAP's musical theater workshop in New York. By the way, my friend, I was still working a full-time job and had a wife and three kids."

"I said that's fucking enough," Gordon yelled. "I'm starting to gag!"

"Then it all stopped! The work stopped, the parties stopped, the newspaper articles stopped, the interviews stopped, the invitations stopped, the contracts stopped, and I stopped!

"Most people expected me to be exactly as I had been and that was never going to happen."

"Did you want to kill them?"

"Sometimes I wanted to punch them in the face, but sometimes their expectations pushed me beyond what I imagined as possible."

"Stop with the abstract bullshit! Give me a concrete example! I cut people like that out of my world. I cut her out of my world. I couldn't put up with her Pollyanna perspective of anything-is-possible-if-you-try-hard-enough attitude.

"Tell me one instance in which somebody's vision of your capabilities raised you up!"

Gordon's continued expressions of anger threw me off guard, especially when he mentioned *her*. It took me an uncomfortable moment to recall an instance that would fit the situation, but he wasn't in the mood for waiting.

"I knew you couldn't think of anything," Gordon shouted. "It was all bullshit, wasn't it?"

"What in hell is making you so crazy? I just had to think for a minute."

"Think on your own time. I don't know how much time I have left!"

"None of us do!"

"You can't think of one, can you? Because there were so many examples that you just can't pick, which one of the ten thousand to choose!" he shouted sarcastically.

"Yes! As a matter of fact, yes!" I cried out. "Lots of people helped me to set a higher goal!"

"One! I want to hear one!"

I picked one out of thin air, hoping it would make him see my perspective. I was shocked at his rage and constant pushing and prodding me to fail at justifying my side of the issue.

"All right! Now shut up! No interruptions! No gastronomic metaphors!

"I'm telling the story no matter what you say or how loud you say it.

"Three weeks after I got out of the hospital in 1995, I was visited by a very talented friend and director, Ray Fulmer, who was planning auditions for *The Lion in Winter*, a remarkable play I'd always wanted to do. In fact, it was the last play your sister did twenty years earlier before she retired from the theater world."

"Get to the fucking point! I'm not going to live forever."

"During the visit with Ray, I had difficulty communicating because many words no longer had meaning to me, and lots of others were too difficult to pronounce with my numb and twisted face. He was patient and kind and gave me the time I needed to respond. But I could see the shock in his eyes."

"Can you see the shock in mine? This is taking too damn long!"

"He'd seen me on stage in leading roles for years: *Working, Man of La Mancha, Rags, Fiddler on the Roof, Joseph and the Amazing Technicolor Dreamcoat, Godspell, The Fantasticks,* and many others.

"I want to hear your story, not your fucking résumé!"

"It must have been difficult for him to see me drool as I struggled to put a simple sentence together."

"Poor baby! Do you know how difficult it is to have no control of my own piss?"

"After an hour, he stood to leave, offering me his hand to shake with my numb knot of fingers, saying, 'I'm expecting to see you at auditions. I can just picture you in the role of the king.' I gave him a crooked smile, and he turned to leave.

"Stop the car. I want to leave too."

"You can leave as soon as I'm done!

"Mary Mooney was in the room as he said, 'Here's the script, Mary, make sure he shows up!' Mary had flown back to the States from Indonesia to assist in my recovery. We had done many theatrical and writing projects together and were close friends. My children called her Aunt Mary and called her husband Uncle John.

"I didn't have fake aunts or uncles! Nobody came to my rescue from Timbuktu or across the street!"

"They came, Gordon, but you wouldn't let them in! Now not another word until I'm finished!

"Mary had a clear idea of who I was and what I was capable of being. She took charge of organizing and implementing a recuperation plan designed specifically for me, pushing me to enunciate every syllable and make myself heard.

"Mary stayed for three months, helping me to learn to speak, playing old recordings of my performances and rehearsing lines.

"I auditioned. I got the role!

"When the curtains parted on opening night, I was almost sick with fear. At the close of the play when the audience stood for a second ovation, I realized I needed to raise my expectations!"

"Well, isn't that just fucking wonderful? Maybe that story should be a Broadway musical. It's got all the makings of a fucking smash hit. You could play the goddamned lead! You could get all the applause you need!"

"Listen, you bastard, I didn't need applause," I yelled back in Gordon's face. "I needed to find myself and lots of other people helped that happen! This story wasn't about me. It was about them! The applause was theirs. It belonged to my wife and my kids and my friends and every soul that raised me up! All the applause was theirs!"

This was one of the only times we ever really fought. We were both loud and angry and vulgar and silenced by the emotional explosion.

A hundred miles must have gone by before he spoke.

"I learned to argue by watching my mother and father. That was their kind of dance. I know all the moves but haven't put them into action for years."

"They fought dirty!"

"I did chase people away," Gordon whispered. "Sony was willing to do anything, and my nurse was ready to sacrifice her life for me.

"I couldn't stand seeing my reflection in their eyes! They saw me through a lens of hope that I didn't share.

"Why did you conjure me up with legs and hands that work? I've been a cripple for years. You'd have been better off arguing with half a person."

"Gordon, I have always seen you as whole! Besides, I had the high expectation that you'd make a fist and punch me."

"Oh, I see! My expectations were too low. You were trying to raise the bar!"

"It was a thought! By the way, if you ever call yourself a cripple again, I'll tie a knot in your catheter!

"Did you mention a bar? I think we need a drink!"

The argument was finished! We started talking about different bars we'd experienced and the stories that went with them.

The anger was behind us, like Texas, a blur in the heat rising off the pavement. Nobody won. Nobody lost. It was just over.

BARS

Gordon talked about some of the bars he frequented while on shore leave with his Navy buddies. The bars had different names but sounded like the same place. There were always a few loose and available women, cheap drinks, and low lights. The music was too loud for conversation, and the air smelled of food fried in overused oil. There was a roughneck bouncer at the door and a baseball bat within easy reach for the bartender. There were a lot of tattoos, paintings of Elvis done on black velvet, and doors ripped off hinges in the restroom. The floors were sticky, air thick with smoke and regulars who called the place home.

I knew the details of traps like this because there are a million of them across the country and around the world. Every guy who ever had a weekend pass from a military base has memories of these places.

"I was in one, years ago, when I saw a guy I recognized from my time in advanced infantry training, sitting at the bar, smoking a pipe.

"I remember his last name was Savage. Last names were all you ever learned in the Army. I made my way over to him, maneuvering though the crowd, ducking mugs of beer and trays heaped with fries and wings.

"I was just about to call out his name when a big guy with his back to me tapped Savage on the shoulder. The moment Savage turned, the guy punched him in the face, driving the stem of the pipe through the back of Savage's throat. The place went crazy. The nightly organized chaos turned into a carnival of brawling bodies, each trying to be the first one out the door. Savage fell backward off the stool and lay on the floor, choking, blood gushing from his mouth and nose and head. The bartender, bat in hand, stood next to me, looking at the body as sirens screamed in the distance.

"'You better beat it, soldier boy, or the cops will have you down at the station for days. I'll handle this. It's my gig! This sucker's name is printed right there on his uniform. That's all they need to know. Now go while you can!'

"I left, walking past bar after bar that looked just like the bar I'd left. Halfway down the block, I heard the screech of cop cars and was glad to be someplace else."

"I always feel like I'm someplace else," Gordon stated with no emotion at all. "Even after all these years in this chair, I have difficulty realizing that this is me right here right now. I feel a bit like that little woodcarving of a cat that's been on the top shelf in my living room. It looks like a cat but that's as far as it goes.

"I had a real cat once. She just showed up one day and was determined to stay. I called her Izzy. I never wanted a pet. I didn't want to be responsible for feedings and shots and vet bills and the daily needs of another life. I chased her away with the whir of my chair a thousand times until I realized that it had become a game that we both enjoyed and so she stayed.

"Izzy would jump up on my lap and sit there for hours, demanding nothing more than a stiff-handed and crude imitation of petting her back. This simple act sent her into ecstasy with purrs and pushes back against the weight of my hand along with rolling stretches.

"I told my sister how much I was enjoying Izzy's company, and for Christmas, she sent me an array of cat toys. Izzy was crazy for them, especially the little stuffed mouse that she would bat with one paw and then the other and send it sailing all over the house.

"My aides didn't like that there was one more thing for them to feed and watch for, but I loved the companionship and overlooked the occasional mishaps and the fact that Izzy fully believed that the living room rug was there for her to sharpen her nails. Even the sound of her claws pulling at the weave gave me pleasure. My home became her home, and she could do what she wanted.

"Izzy would let me know with a whine or meow when she needed to go outside where she'd relieve herself along the fence line in the sandy soil. I'd respond quickly to her call and roll my chair to the door and let her exit or enter. She gave me purpose and that felt good!

"She'd sleep by my side, filling up that empty space with yawns and licks and the occasional pounce onto a newly spotted toy. I was constantly aware of her movements, and she was aware of mind. It was comforting and helped the house to feel like a home.

"For fourteen years, Izzy and I repeated our daily routines and then one September morning, I let her out, and she never came back! I searched the yard in all her favorite places but not a trace was found. I rolled around the neighborhood sidewalks for days in hopes of spotting her. I left the sliding glass door open wide enough for Izzy to come and find me, but she never did.

"I suspect she might have died. I have no idea how old she was when she showed up on my deck years earlier. I even thought that perhaps she went looking for a hand that could pet her in long firm strokes and toss stuffed toys for her to scamper after.

"At any rate, eventually, I decided she'd given me all she could, and I'd done the same for her.

"When Sony heard of my loss, she sent me a kitten-sized wooden carving of a cat. It was very beautiful and a real piece of art, but it made me sad. It was stiff and unyielding to my touch, reminding me too much of my own situation—still, paralyzed, and powerless. I asked my aide to place it high on a shelf, out of reach, where it can't be seen and that is where it stays. So much like myself!"

"I see you, Gordon."

"Yes, and you let me see the world, and I am grateful! Now let me see another bar. Let your words be the alcohol for my addiction."

"Do you have an addiction?

"Only to your stories! The alcohol I consume is just a little medicine to help me get through the blue days."

"Do you have many of those?"

"Not when you're around."

"Do you have another bar story? That little peek into my soft side needs to be contrasted with something that has a little bit of zing in it."

"I do, but it's about a different kind of bar than the ones we've talked about before. This one I'd grown to love and one I also walked away from because I loved it too much. Are you interested?"

"Oh, that bar! I remember the first time you told me about that place. Let's see how it holds up as a rerun."

"It's a long one!"

"There's a shitload of road in front of us. Let it rip!"

MR. MIKE'S

"Syracuse was a nightclub town, halfway between Toronto and the Big Apple. There was great music and real dance floors in these places. The best one in the city was called Mr. Mike's. It had class! I snuck in one night just to check it out. I got bounced within minutes but not before getting an eyeful.

"It looked like something out of a 1930s movie musical from MGM. Just past the coat check and maître d', there were three carpeted steps that lead down to the dim lights of the main room. I could see about twenty tables, surrounding a half-circle dance floor. Beyond that, there was a large raised stage for the orchestra. The wall behind them was all mirrors, making the room look like it went on forever. To the left was a polished mahogany bar with about fifteen black leather stools. Each stool had a cushioned backrest embossed with the letter M. Shiny brass rails and chrome details were everywhere along with soft light filtered through milk-glass globes that hung from the ceiling.

"There was the sound of the music, clashing with the subtle scrape and squeak of silverware against china. I could see a haze of tobacco smoke in the air and smell rare steak on the grill along with expensive perfume dabbed behind every diamond-studded ear.

"To the right of the stage were the restrooms, private offices, and swinging doors to the kitchen. There were servers carrying silver trays crisscrossing the room in all directions, all quietly dancing to the chef's rhythm. The whole scene made me smile!

"Unfortunately, the guys at the front door weren't going to let a fifteen-year-old inside a place like this. I kept trying though. And failing! Eventually, I learned by watching from a distance about the attitude and attire needed for my next attempt. I dressed up in a good suit, white shirt, and tie. I polished my shoes, slicked back my hair, and slipped in behind some legitimate customers. It helped that I looked older than my age and was tall, thanks to a recent growth spurt. The next challenge was to find someone to dance with. This wasn't so easy! Most people came in couples, and the women that didn't have an escort looked like they had business of another kind.

"Customers sat at tables with pressed tablecloths, fresh flowers, scented candles, gold-rimmed china, and menus that read like a European travelogue. This wasn't the school cafeteria! The music came from a live orchestra, and when people danced, there was no shimmying. It was the cha-cha or rumba or waltz.

"I stood with my back against the wall near the door to the men's room for about thirty minutes, barely being noticed. After a while, I thought I'd better duck inside and hide from the suspicious headwaiter. A tall muscled man in a tailored black suit and bowtie about forty-five or so was at the sink, washing his hands. He looked up, saw me in the mirror, and asked gruffly, 'Hey, kid, what are you doing here?'

"'Dancing,' I said, pretending like I was a regular as I turned my back on him to use the urinal.

"'How old are you? Never mind. I don't want to know. You look just about old enough! Can you dance?' he questioned with interest.

"'Yeah! I told you! I come here to dance!' I said with a little forced irritation in my voice.

"'Can you dance with a woman a'—he drew on a thick dark cigar that had rested on the edge of the sink and then continued—'a few years older than you?' he inquired, like it was an interview.

"'I can dance with anybody,' I said as I washed my hands and turned to grab a towel.

"'Are you alone?' he questioned, walking around me, sizing me up.

"'Yeah, I'm alone for the moment,' I said as if ten women at the bar were waiting for me. 'And I know how to take care of myself, too, just in case you have any funny ideas!'

"He grunted out a short laugh, ending with 'You look good, kid.' Then he continued as if we were about to sign a contract. 'Listen! A lady friend of mine and I are with a couple of business associates at table number three. She's been bugging me to dance all night. I am not the dancing type! You know what I mean? I'll give you fifty bucks if you take her for a spin around the floor for a while.'

"He stepped toward me with a little a smirk on his face, never blinking. He stopped about a handshake's distance away, but there was no handshake. I did not back up or turn away or lose eye contact. My mother taught me to hold my ground, and he seemed to appreciate that.

"'It's table number three. She's wearing a red dress,' he said, pushing fifty bucks into my coat pocket. 'Wait a couple of minutes and then stop by, like we know each other, like you're helping me out around the club. What's your name?'

"'Dave,' I said. 'My name is Dave.'

"'I'm Mike, Dancing Dave,' he said with a laugh as he pushed the door open. 'Mr. Mike, as in the owner of this joint,' he added as the door closed slowly behind him.

"That's how it began. Mike introduced me at lots of tables over the years. There were lots of red dresses. Lots!

"I was finally making money by dancing! It wasn't on Broadway or leaping across the big screen, like Gene Kelly, but it was good money. Besides, *Goldfinger* was the movie that was speaking to my generation. Blockbuster musicals were on their way out. It was just as well! I felt a little bit like James Bond at the moment and used his 007 persona the best I could. I wondered if I could pull off the impersonation and asked Mike one day when I saw him alone at the bar.

"'People believe what they want to believe! It's up to you to make them believe you're who you pretend to be. I think you have the knack,' Mike said.

"It was hard to get out of the house that first year or so. My mother would not have understood my off-the-record, under-the-table income. She was way too sick. I didn't want her to worry over me, so I hid everything. This new world of mine was getting farther from that waxed kitchen floor and harder to get to.

"I hid my nightclub clothes in a trunk, tucked under a tarp in the shed I'd used as a clubhouse when I was a boy. I'd retrieve them and dress in the dark after scrambling out my bedroom window, crawling across the porch roof and climbing down an overhanging tree. Then it was a short bike ride to the club. I came in the employee's entrance at Mr. Mike's and discreetly cleaned myself up a bit in the men's room before making my entrance.

"Jake, the bartender, always kept the stool closest to the dance floor open for me. He'd pour a ginger ale over lots of ice along with a slice of lime and slide it into my hand.

"'It looks just like everybody else's drink,' I said to Jake under my breath.

"'Any liquid that doesn't contain alcohol is just piss,' he responded with a wink. I could always count on Jake for a creative description. He used to dance, too, but not at Mr. Mike's. He once sang and danced on Broadway. Not in any leading roles but chorus-type stuff until arthritis made him park his dancing shoes.

"Jake still had Broadway in his heart! He'd go to see shows as often he could and then share his complete theatrical review while I waited with my ginger ale for my next partner. His critiques were a show in themselves filled with colorful language and sexual details.

"He said he worked at Mr. Mike's because of seeing the musical *Hello, Dolly!*, adding that it had given him an appreciation of cleavage!

"To the side of my drink, a few bucks always appeared for the bartender. I never knew where they came from. My pay was delivered in the breast pocket of my suit coat, or hidden in a handshake. It wasn't talked about. The fee was never discussed. It was variable, depending on the situation, the time, the woman, and her man. I watched for signals from the table. Sometimes the gentleman would stand up, walk over, and cut in. That's when I knew the job was finished. Sometimes they'd flash me five fingers or ten or twenty, meaning keep dancing. Sometimes they'd point to the bar where I'd take the lady for a drink as I sipped ginger ale.

"I quickly learned that I had to talk as well as dance. It wasn't so hard. After all, I did grow up in a house with three women! It was like dancing: the leading question, followed by a natural response and necessary smile. I kept up with the current movies, which were always a topic I could stretch out to fill an entire conversation. I read the newspaper that was delivered to our house every day. That helped! I knew enough to stay clear of personal stuff—too much truth, politics, and religion.

"Mike used to say, 'A smart man knows everything and has an opinion on nothing.'

"Of course, Jake had an opinion on club discourse and added, "Women like to talk. A woman would rather talk than have sex. Talk is verbal foreplay! Women want to be talked into bed."

"'Not these women,' Mike warned, slowly waving one of his fingers at me, his manicured fingernail gleaming like a polished candlestick.

"Periodically, one of my partners would press a few bucks into my hand. Many of them were fully aware of what the deal was and liked it. They liked showing off for the guy with the wallet. There were also those who were bored with the table talk. Some wanted more than a dance! They would rub their body against me, play with the hair on the nape of my neck, drop a shoulder strap, or whisper their number in my ear. There was one number I wrote down and kept for weeks. If it got too intense, I'd signal Jake who'd interrupt, saying, 'I got a phone call.' Sometimes Jake would just tap me on the shoulder with the message because I'd get a little lost in the moment. Mr. Mike said, 'That's what caused the last guy who could dance to suddenly disappear,' then he laughed that laugh I'd come to know and puffed on his cigar. I threw that number out!

"Jake gave me a silent nod, and after Mike walked away, adding to the story while refreshing my drink. 'You're dancing with the devil, kid. Don't let the laugh fool you.'

"I saw lots of money change hands at the club that had nothing to do with me or drinks or food.

"Guys in expensive suits would come and go, dropping off and picking up envelopes of all sizes. Mike would thumb though the contents, nod his approval, and write in a little notebook he kept in his vest pocket.

"One night, one of the suits gave me an envelope for Mike. I walked across the dance floor, handed it to Mike, and pointed back to the guy who'd given it to me. Mike was pissed! He ordered me to follow him as he jumped up and walked directly to the guy. Mike pushed him into his office, grabbed the lapels of the guy's suit, and backed him up against the wall.

"'Hey, Mike, I was just trying to—' the guy pleaded.

"'Try harder!' Mike interrupted, slapping him across the face with the hand holding the envelope. The envelope split open, sending hundred-dollar bills fanning out across the floor. 'This kid is clean! Do you hear that? He's clean! He's going to stay clean until I say different. If you got business with me, it's with me and nobody else!'

"Mike never said a thing to me about the incident. I suspected he wanted me to see how things worked, but I went to Jake for an explanation. Back at the bar, Jake kept his head down as if he was trying to wipe a stain off the counter and whispered a few words to me.

"'I serve drinks, Dancing Dave. That's my job. Nobody asks me to do shit because why? Because I'm the bartender! Your job is to dance. The minute you think it's something else or let somebody make it something else, everything changes. When someone waiting for a drink asks me if it's icy out, I say, 'Do I look like a weatherman? The only ice I know comes in a glass.' It can be slippery around here, kid. Watch where you step! You're just on the brink of becoming the man you're pretending to be. Give yourself time to get there. It's like driving. Watch the speed limit and think about how to get around a tricky situation. Always look three car lengths ahead.'

"Jake dished out his philosophy like he was serving beer nuts, common sense, free for the taking.

"I took a handful!"

TRAIN RUNNER

"That phrase, common sense, needs to be updated," Gordon said with some irritation.

"What do you mean?"

"Common sense is not common at all. It's rare! Most people have no idea what sound judgment is. They just act without thinking and then spend most of their life dealing with the consequences."

"What brought this topic to the forefront?"

"That fucking phrase. I hate it! You're an educator! Why isn't common sense taught in school? Unlike algebra, this subject could be put to use every day for the rest of somebody's life."

"Don't try to push that onto teachers! Schools can't teach common sense! Life teaches that curriculum! Those lessons are out in the world and are taught through experiences and opportunities to fail as well as succeed. It requires some element of risk. That knowledge comes to the learner incrementally through thousands of interactions with others, exposure to diversity, travel, and hands-on genuine living."

"Did you allow your sons to take risks, or is this an untested train of thought?"

"Allow it? I promoted it. You can't expect a bird to know how to fly by talking about flight. That's just an abstract concept until he takes that leap or you push him off the branch."

"As a parent, didn't that scare the hell out of you?"

"Not as much as the thought of them not taking risks at all."

"Did any of them get hurt, suffer pain, get scared, or have losses?"

"Every single one! They also healed, recovered, got over it, and gained the knowledge necessary to risk more, fly higher, and live large! They learned to be resilient!"

"I was kept in a box by people who lived in a box. I was totally unprepared for flight. When I got out and joined the Navy, I was an inexperienced fledgling and vulnerable. My common sense didn't exist, and my judgment was flawed. I had not done enough, seen enough, or learned enough to navigate the real world."

"Didn't you leap out of sheer frustration, hunger for change, or desire?"

"No, and nobody pushed me off the branch. I think I just fell into the Navy!"

"It's not easy to push, or even let a child try their wings. It's scary and dangerous and causes endless hours of sleepless nights."

"Tell me about a time when you let one of your sons venture into the unknown. Take me there."

"Gordon, it's no one thing. It's a thousand things, and it starts from day one! First they crawl, then baby steps, hanging on to your hand or furniture, then they walk, and soon they run, and then they fly. There are lots of bumps and bruises along the way."

"Don't give me a by-the-numbers set of instructions or philosophy on child-rearing! Give me a story."

"Okay, I'll tell you a story about Josh. He was fourteen, and we were backpacking in Europe. We were on an old and overcrowded train heading into Athens. Starting about thirty miles outside the city, every time we stopped at a station, train runners would hop on the train and go from car to car, looking for travelers who might need a room in Athens.

"They each carried brochures and flyers and business cards along with a chart showing nightly or weekly rates. Many of the runners were college students or free-spirited travelers who were paid a stipend for bringing visitors to the different establishments.

"They needed to be skilled in salesmanship and multiple languages if possible. I understood this routine, and when I heard one of them say there was one room left at the Hotel Capri, I waved him over. I knew where this place was located and thought it would be a great central location for our sightseeing.

"The runners would ride the train all the way into the city and then walk their clients to their hotels where the runners would be paid, or given floor space to sleep.

"Josh and I planned on reaching our destination on a Thursday evening because arriving on a Friday would generally mean that all the good and affordable rooms were already booked for the weekend. I'd learned this years earlier when traveling with Terry and Sony.

"Josh loved the excitement of all these young people hopping on the train, running through the cars, selling rooms, and hopping off again to run to another train car before the conductor could catch them and demand a ticket. He saw it as a fast-moving game that he wanted to play. Josh only knew English but was animated enough to pull it off if given a chance.

"As the sun set, our salesman, Alec, walked us through the crowded streets of Athens past the gyro stands and open markets and to the Hotel Carpi, which was probably quite grand eighty years ago. The plaster and windows were cracked, elevator no longer worked, and it looked like the set for a film noir murder scene, but it was perfect for us.

"Josh and Alec talked the entire way about where Josh and I had traveled and what we hoped to do in Athens. Alec said that a music festival was happening on Saturday night and that more train runners might be needed to handle the incoming crowd.

"Josh and I hauled our backpacks to the third floor, got cleaned up a little, and then took the stairs to the rooftop bar. There, we sipped ouzo and looked out over the city to where the sound-and-light show was bringing the Parthenon to life. We also met about a dozen other train runners who were camping out on the roof for three drachmas a night, or free if they brought in enough paying customers.

"It was a magical night of international storytelling, laughter, and ouzo. I loved seeing my fourteen-year-old son immerse himself in communication with people from all over the world and share his stories of backpacking across France, Switzerland, and Italy.

"Eventually, we hit the streets for some lamb kebabs, pita bread, and a short walk in the sea-filled night air before sleep.

"In the morning, we headed to the acropolis to explore the Parthenon, the iconic Athenian temple and ruins from the fifth century BC—the temple monument, grounds, and the architecture that is still copied all over the world. This was followed by the Plaka, two museums, and finally, the famous flea market where Josh asked to go on his own for a while.

"'Sure,' I said, wanting him to explore by himself. 'I'm going to sit in the shade at this café and have some Greek wine. Find me here when you're done.'"

"That was it?" Gordon interrupted. "His being pushed off the branch was a little bit of shopping at a flea market while Daddy sat nearby?"

"Let me finish! I made sure he had some extra money and asked if he knew his way back to the hotel. He answered, 'Of course, and I have a city map!' he added as he wandered into the crowd. Ten minutes later, he returned with six of the train runners we'd met on the roof the night before, breathlessly explaining that they needed another runner and asked if he could fill the spot.

"Lots of things ran through my head like how I was going to explain to my wife that I had lost our son in a foreign country, or questions like what if he gets caught without a ticket, or what if he misses the train out there in one of those towns outside Athens? All that and more was swirling in my head while Josh and the runners stood there, anxiously waiting for my response.

"'Try to be back by one in morning. I'll be on the roof, waiting to hear all the stories.' Josh threw his arms around me for a quick hug in front of everyone and then they all rushed off, disappearing into the marketplace crowd.

"At twenty after one in the morning, he returned and talked my ear off with story upon story of jumping on and off trains, selling rooms to people from all over the world, running from conductors, getting lost and finding his way back, and meeting cute teenage girls from Amsterdam.

"The sun was rising when he fell asleep on my shoulder. I did not sleep. I just stroked his head, thanking God he was safe and thinking about the wonderful man he was becoming. I slept later when he left to meet up with those girls."

"Did you pay for all those trips with your kids?"

"I paid for the one when they were four, but they had to pay for their teenage trip."

"How'd they earn the money?"

"The same way I made money when I was a kid. They had to hustle—get out there in the world and find a way.

They did all kinds of odd jobs to make a buck: wash windows, clean up construction sites, wash and wax cars, mowing, raking, and a thousand other things. Every penny went into the bank, and they knew that it was up to them if they wanted the adventure to happen.

"What they didn't know was that all those struggles for every penny and those interactions with adults and others helped prepare them emotionally as much as it did financially. It taught them the power of having a goal and working toward it. By the time we got on the plane, they were more than ready for the larger world."

"When did you realize that your mother and father had done the same for you but in a different way?"

"I grew to understand that particular enlightened perspective in bits and pieces over the years. There was no one revelation. There was a slow and growing confidence with every risk I took and thankfulness for their parenting and love."

"Did you ever thank them?"

"A thousand times!"

"I never said shit to my father. I regret that! By the time I had enough sense to put the words together, he was gone. As for my mother, you got to know her when she was at her very best. She visited me in California once during that time of sobriety, but she was a stranger to me. I liked who she'd become. I think that person would have made a good mother."

"Wilma probably thought the same thing."

"She spent the week reminiscing, talking about the cartoons I used to draw as a child and how they made her laugh. I didn't realize she looked at them, liked them, or even reacted to them. I don't remember her laughing! I wish I did.

"She talked about birthday cakes she baked for me, standing little plastic figures in the frosting that I would later play with for hours on the living room floor.

"She also mentioned a set of drafting tools that my father bought for me one Christmas when I was sixteen because I was good at mechanical drawing and measurements. I remember unwrapping the case and looking at the finely crafted set of compasses, drafting scales, triangles, inch and metric rulers along with other things for precise calculations and accurate drawings. I never even took them out of the box. Anger paralyzed me, made me blind."

"But you see now."

"Now it's too late!

"David, what were you like at sixteen?"

"I was probably just as blind! It has a lot to do with being young. True vision comes when you can see things from a distance and in context. Seeing a tree by itself is far different from seeing it in a field of other trees. Comparisons and contrasts help give sight clarity. I think that attitude and perspective have a lot to do with how we see things. Sometimes we only see what we're looking for. At sixteen, my vision wasn't exactly focused. I spent a lot of time seeing what wasn't there and missed some things that were right in front of me."

"Take me there. Let one of your stories paint the picture of the teenage you. Don't show me the varnished version that you're so good at projecting to the rest of the world. I want to see the pimples and beginnings of worry lines. Give me some of your missteps, mistakes, screw ups, and scars."

SIXTEEN

"When I turned sixteen, the first thing I wanted to do was to get my driver's permit. My father gave me lessons in what we called the new car. The new car was a used 1956 Plymouth. It was better than the old car, a 1948 Dodge but not by much. The new car was rusted out along the wheel wells, rocker panels, and headlights. It was a four-door model with a three-speed standard shift on the column. This car had windows that actually went up and down when you cranked them and a radio that worked most of the time. There was nothing sexy about this ride, but it served its purpose.

"My father was an excellent driving instructor. He knew and obeyed all the rules while he made sure I knew why I was doing what I was doing at all times. He taught me how to fit in to the flow of the traffic and warned me to look further ahead than the car in front of me. He said, 'Looking three cars ahead lets you know what's going on and gives you time to react.'

"I wanted to tell him that Jake had told me the same thing but decided to keep my two worlds apart. I took that lesson into many areas of my life.

"While we were in the car, he'd tell me war stories in between practical information regarding turn signals and braking time. He also told me that he'd finally saved the money to order his very first new car and that it would be coming in a few weeks. I loved hearing the excitement in his voice. He never got anything new. He sounded like a kid waiting for Christmas.

"I was glad money was loosening up and that he had time for my little sister. He and my mother would take her camping or to the amusement park or even to visit family in Massachusetts. He'd ask me to go, but it was too late for me. I'd moved on and grown up without him. I knew it wasn't his fault, but in some way, his asking made me angry. Even when he'd ask me to go fishing, I made up lame excuses. I think I wanted to hurt him the way he hurt me. 'I'm busy, Dad. I've got plans. No thanks!'

"When Mr. Mike heard about my learning how to drive, he said, 'Take my Lincoln out for a spin.'

"It was brand new and garage kept, had all the bells and whistles, jet black and about a mile long.

"'I haven't got my license yet,' I said, catching the keys he tossed. 'What if I get pulled over by the cops?'

"This really made Mike laugh. 'Nobody pulls Mr. Mike's car over,' he said. 'If they do, I'll tell them you stole it.'

"I think he was kidding, but I didn't get pulled over, so I never knew for sure. I loved that car—its smell, leather seats, waxed finish, and low rumble of the eight-cylinder engine. It had power windows, air-conditioning, and a stereo system better than what was in most homes. He never let anybody touch his car but me.

"The day I discovered my license in the mailbox, my father's new car was in the driveway. It had been delivered while I was at school. I walked around the car, inspecting every polished detail. I opened the door and sat behind the wheel. The keys were in the ignition, just waiting for me.

"Without much thought, I turned the key of this boxy beige Rambler Ambassador. It wasn't what one would call a cool car, but it was new. I put it into reverse and carefully backed down the driveway, slipped it into drive, and headed up to route eleven. I was just going to take it around the block and then back to the driveway.

"Following all my father's instructions, I used my turn signals, looked ahead, and I came to a complete stop at the red light. That's when I heard the screeching of brakes behind me and felt the jolt as the entire back of my father's brand-new car was crushed into the rear seat. After the cops left and the car was towed away, I walked home and into the house.

"'Did you see your father's new car?' my mother yelled from her bedroom.

"'I did,' I yelled back.

"'What do you think?' she asked, crossing the kitchen in her bathrobe to look out the window. 'It's gone!' she exclaimed. 'It's not there!'

"I thought about saying it must have been stolen but confessed.

"'Better call your father,' she said, handing me the phone. He's probably just about ready to leave the bus garage. I dialed. It rang. He answered.

"'Hi, Dad. It's me, Dave.'

"'Hello! Are you calling about my new car? Is it in the driveway? It's a beauty, isn't it? I was sure you'd like it. When I get home, we'll—'

"'Dad,' I interrupted, and I told him exactly what happened. There was a long silence before he spoke.

"'Are you hurt?' he asked.

"'No, but the car is—'

"'Don't worry about it,' he said. 'It's only a car.'

"I never felt so close to my father as that moment.

"I told Jake what happened. He said, 'If you were my kid, I'd buy another car and use it to run you over.' Then he smacked me on the side of my head with a menu.

"The second thing I did when I turned sixteen was to find an afterschool job in a bank downtown. The lady in personnel got my age wrong, and I didn't correct her. She thought I was a junior in college, not high school. So did my boss's red-haired secretary! By the time my boss found out, he said I was too valuable to let go. The hours were from four to eight, which left me available for Mr. Mike's. The bank job enabled me to buy a used car without being questioned about where the money came from. I also bought my mother a washer, a dryer, a color television set, and a wig.

"The wig helped to hide the negative effects of her recent chemo treatments. My folks thought it was amazing how much money I could make after school.

"I was flying under the radar screen because my mother was dancing with cancer. Her partner would come and go and come again, disrupting the household, making me nearly invisible. Now my suit hung like a billboard from a hook in my bedroom. I washed and dressed in the bathroom, walked out the front door, and drove to the club. Late at night, I'd kneel by mother's bed, rhythmically stroking her feverish forehead, telling her lies, 'School's going great! I've got lots of friends. No, I'm not tired a bit.'

"My mother drank tea. When she was feeling well enough, we'd sit in our tiny little kitchen with our hands cupped around mugs of hot water, dunking Lipton's tea bags and talking. During moments like this, I'd forget she was sick at all. I loved hearing the New England accent that she never lost. All her words seemed gentle compared to the hard nasal sound of New Yorkers. She was filled with expression. Even her eyes talked as she told stories of growing up in a family with twelve children. I think she was a tomboy from the stories she shared. She liked adventure and travel and once dated a guy that flew a biplane in an air show. She said, 'There was hardly anything more thrilling than flying in an open cockpit during a full loop, except dancing with your father!'"

Furniture

"I could use a little of that biplane air right now! It's frigging hot in here," Gordon yelled. "I'm used to freezing my ass off in the hospital and begging for more blankets. Now I'm begging for air-conditioning! If the weather had been more cooperative, you could have taken the northern route through the Rockies, dropping south after Albuquerque."

"Then you would have wanted a coat, and you'd be complaining about the heater not being hot enough."

"Am I like that?"

"No, I was kidding. You almost never complain, and I'm trying to learn how you manage that."

"You really want to know?"

"Sure. Let me in on the secret."

"Okay, but you're not going to like it. I generally don't complain because I have learned to accept whatever is before me. If cereal is served, and I wanted bacon and eggs, I eat cereal! If my aide dresses me in a wool sweater and khakis, but I wanted a blue pullover and jeans, I wear what he puts on me. I just stopped caring!"

"Not when I dress you! When I'm at the closet with you in charge, it's always 'No, not that one. The other one, and I look better in blue.'"

"That's because I like bossing you around, and you're such a sucker. If I play the quad card, I can get you to do just about anything."

"You ass! You're playing me right now, aren't you?"

"You bet! And I'm loving it!" he said while laughing. "I don't know many people well enough to be totally myself during conversations, or even arguments. I can be a little sarcastic and over the top, you know, even a bit vulgar!"

"You don't have to tell me that!"

"You see, people don't expect someone in a chair to disagree, be funny or rude or have an opinion, or brains or even a personality. To most people, I'm not a person with feelings and a history. They see me as an extension of the chair. To them, I'm just an awkward piece of furniture."

"If you're a piece of furniture, I'm a match to the set!"

"That's why we're brothers."

"Following the stroke, I became invisible to most and an annoyance to many. Once, when I was being transported from the emergency room to the x-ray department, I was hurriedly put on the gurney and left alone in the hallway. In their rush to move me, they didn't notice I'd been placed with my left arm awkwardly twisted under my body. While lying there, under the bright fluorescent lights, I tried to get the attention of anyone who passed by to help me. A woman noticed my struggle to be heard and my unsuccessful attempt to speak. As she leaned over the gurney, I carefully tried to express my situation. None of the words were coming out correctly, and I was choking on my own drool. We held eye contact until her husband pulled her away, saying, 'Don't worry about him. He's probably retarded.' I could give you a thousand examples like this."

"Don't bother. I've got my own. If you were a piece of furniture, describe yourself to me."

"I don't know, maybe a used oak, kitchen chair with pieces that have been glued together a hundred times. I creak and wobble a bit, but I'm still a good sit."

"I'm an oversized, out-of-date, and very rickety stuffed recliner with worn piss-stained fabric barely covering broken springs."

"I take it that your description is not open for discussion."

"That is correct, but we can discuss your doing something about this heat!"

"I'll tell you about a snowstorm in upstate New York. That will cool you down."

"Go for it. It's not air-conditioning, but it's better than nothing. Why didn't you have that fucker fixed before you left?"

"No fucking time, my friend. No time!"

BABY, IT'S COLD OUTSIDE

"Syracuse has always been known as the buckle on the snow-belt. Storm after storm whip across the region from late October to early April. Winds called Alberta clippers blow down from Canada and across the Great Lakes where they gather up all kinds of moisture. Then they dump lake-effect snow again and again, transforming my old stomping ground.

"There were no hard edges after a storm. Everything was softened by drifting snow that piled up on rooftops, like white pillows and extra quilts.

"When I was a kid, every snowfall meant money. I'd grab a shovel and go house to house, selling my services. It was hard work, but I liked how easy it was to measure progress. Each shovel full, tossed on top of the snowbank resulted in clear evidence of where I was in relation to the goal. I gave all that up when I started work at the bank where I sat entering numbers into machines, hoping for a correct balance at the end of the night.

"During the winter of 1966, there was a snowstorm that crippled the entire city. I had arrived at work just as the storm reached blizzard status. By eight that night, all hope of getting home was out of the question. Roads were closing and visibility was virtually zero along with the plunging temperature. I had already decided to stay at the bank for the night when my boss's secretary made me a better offer.

"'Listen!' she said, leaning over my desk in her V-neck sweater. 'I just heard the latest forecast. They're predicting over one hundred inches of snow to fall! The phones are down, and they've told us not to use the elevator because they expect the power to fail. When that goes, the heat goes. Do you really want to stay here? I live about sixteen blocks away. It will be a hell of a walk, but I've got lots of blankets and a couch in my apartment.'

"We bundled up the best we could by putting old newspapers under our clothes and wrapping ourselves in everything we could find in the lost-and-found box in the break room. We looked like a couple of hillbillies with oversized coats, mismatched gloves, and layers of plaid-and-striped scarves tied every which way around our bodies.

"Our laughter over the spontaneous costume party brought the security guard running. He thought we looked like we belonged on *The Red Skeleton Show*, a popular TV program specializing in comic skits.

"The lights went out just as we were coming down the stairwell. As soon as the bank door closed and locked behind us, we questioned the wisdom of our decision. The snow was way above our knees and wind so strong that we had to hold on to each other just to walk.

"There were no cars, no lights, no beeping horns, and no traffic signals. There were just the sounds of howling winds around us and sirens in the distance. In places where we were unprotected by buildings, there were six-foot drifts that we climbed over and sometimes fell down, laughing like we were ten-year-olds. We each had a couple of awkward slips but no injuries.

"The whole world was soft. Cold but soft! At one point, the scarf I had tied around my face blew up over my head and was gone. She steadied herself in front of me and carefully reworked another scarf to do the same job, saying, 'Can't let anything happen to that face.'

"It took an hour and a half, but we finally made it to her second-floor apartment in an old Victorian house on James Street. I had never been there before and was surprised to be greeted by two little boys and their babysitter who lived downstairs. After apologizing for the lateness and explaining the circumstances, she said goodbye to the sitter and turned, saying, 'Yup, they're mine! The little guy on the couch is three, and this one helping me with my coat is five. He thinks he's the man of the house.'

"'I am the man of the house,' said the older boy, giving me a rather hateful look as he carried her coat down the hall.

"'Is there another man of the house?' I asked, not knowing just how relaxed I should get.

"'Not anymore,' she answered, adding, 'I hate it when my mother is right!'

"After dumping the rest of her odd ensemble, which the kids said looked funny, she tucked them into bed and returned with more candles and a bathrobe for me.

"'This was his,' she said, laying it over the back of a chair. 'Get out of those wet things while I change.'

"By the time she returned in her housecoat, I had the extra candles lit, and my clothes draped over the backs of furniture. She pulled out a bottle of Southern Comfort, saying, 'This was his too.'

"'Janis Joplin's favorite drink,' I said, filling two short glasses. 'I love that rock and roller. Does he like Janis?'

"'Oh, he likes Janis and Debbie and Sarah and all the girls, if you get my drift! They don't even have to sing.'

"We sat on the couch, sharing a wool blanket, sipping Southern Comfort in the glow of the candles. She didn't let me hide in talk of movies and front-page bullet points. I didn't know whether it was the Southern Comfort we were sipping, the wool blanket we were under, or the warmth of our conversation, but suddenly, anything seemed possible.

"I even told her about Mr. Mike's. She told me about getting involved in a relationship that she knew was bad for her. I didn't ask questions. She said she was trying to find a way out but didn't know how. I understood and comforted her with a supportive hug that turned into an embrace and a kiss, which lead to other comforts under the blanket.

"Multiple hours passed. We didn't know the snow had stopped. We didn't know the plows were running and streets were opening. We didn't know the electricity was restored. We were lost in candlelit honesty and sleep. It felt good!

"Suddenly, the door burst open! Startled, we both looked up to see our boss in his snow-covered overcoat and frostbitten expression. He just stood there, staring at us in our housecoats and blanket, in the candlelight surrounded by discarded clothes and an empty bottle of booze. It looked far worse than it was.

"There was no reasoning with him. No logical explanation was going to make a difference. He'd already summed up the situation with a mix of embarrassment and guilt, ordering me to get dressed. I did right there in front of them both. I wasn't about to leave her alone with him. He gave me a ride home. Talk about awkward!

"The deal was this: He wouldn't tell my parents if I didn't tell his wife. It worked for me!

"I think my friend found the way out she was looking for."

HIGH SCHOOL
GRADUATIONS

"Now let me see you at sixteen, Gordon. I don't need to see the pimples!"

"When I turned sixteen, I got a part-time job at a local gas station. It was not as upscale as your bank job, but it did have its benefits, though none of them included a secretary in a V-neck sweater.

"It was back in the day when a fill-up came with Green Stamps, a windshield wash, tire pressure, oil check. The pay was minimal, but I got to meet people from all over the country who pulled off the highway for gas and a clean restroom.

"Yes, I had to clean the crapper, but it got me out of the house!

"It gave me the chance to hear different accents and points of view. Best of all, it offered me the opportunity to see all kinds of cars. Being from that particular part of Texas, most people drove pickup trucks, and usually, they were Fords, Chevrolets, or Dodges. Nine times out of ten, they were dirty, dented, rusted out, and burning oil. I got all excited to see the occasional Corvette, Mustang, or Jaguar. I loved it when some guy with a cool car needed air in a tire and would ask me to pull it over to the air pump while he was taking a piss.

"I remember the first time I ever sat in the bucket seat of a Plymouth Barracuda. This two-door hard-top pony car stole my heart! It had a wraparound rear window and lots of power. It was my dream car, and though my parents thought I was saving everything for college, the Barracuda was my goal, and every dime went into making that goal a reality. Midway through my senior year at San Angelo Central High in 1968, I spent all my savings, birthday, and Christmas money on buying a lightly used Barracuda.

"It was my breakout moment of temporary independence, but it didn't go down well with my mother who called me an idiot! It didn't matter.

"My classmates called me Barracuda Man, which mattered a lot.

"By the time graduation rolled around, I knew I needed to get further away than where that car could take me. I also was struggling to feed the eight hungry cylinders hidden under that Barracuda's hood.

"Were you ready when your graduation finally rolled around?"

"Hardly! At the end of my senior year of high school, I was voted best dancer. They hung a picture of me in the hallway along with pictures of the class clown, class couple, most likely to succeed, and all the rest. The same pictures were printed in the yearbook.

"We, the graduating class, called ourselves Trix of 66. How weird to have a cartoon character that plugged breakfast cereal as our class mascot! I did a pen-and-ink drawing of that little rabbit. It also ended up in the yearbook. I would have rather drawn Tony the Tiger, but they said it didn't rhyme.

"High school graduation snuck up on me. Other graduates had made plans and were heading off to college or joining the Army, or even getting married. Marriage is what my dancing girlfriend wanted. She was the one I'd met at my first high school dance. She believed that all those spins and turns would lead us to the altar. She was wrong. Marriage was the absolute last thing on my mind. It was too grown-up, too permanent, too confining, too duty filled, and way too predictable! I never did like a dance that required exact steps. I was more the freestyle guy. We broke up! We never danced together again. I missed that more than I missed her.

"I spent the summer attending an arts program at Syracuse University. My parents gave this to me as a graduation present. I was shocked! This was not at all within my parent's realm of thinking or their budget. Later, I found out that the girl across the street was attending the same set of classes, and her father offered to pay for my tuition if I'd drive her back and forth each day.

"The experience opened my eyes to all kinds of possibilities. I'd never taken school seriously. Neither of my parents went beyond the eighth grade and never talked about college. I had been a business major in high school only because it seemed the easiest way to get through it, not because I was interested. Also, Mike always said. 'The ones that end up on top are the ones who can handle numbers.'

"Jake said, 'Being on top all the time can be boring,' but I didn't get the joke at the time.

"At the end of the summer, I was offered a scholarship at the SU school of architecture but couldn't accept it because I'd never taken any of the necessary college prep classes in high school.

"The idea of going to college rushed over me like a tidal wave. It scared me and thrilled me at the same time. I kept thinking that maybe college was the ticket to someplace I'd been looking for. I felt desperate!

"I went back to see my high school guidance counselor and asked if I could return for one more year to take the necessary classes. He took my request to the school board, and because I was still only seventeen, they said yes. But there were conditions. My counselor informed me that I'd have to take French I, French II, algebra, geometry, and physics all at the same time. He said it would be nearly impossible but that I could try. I always liked a challenge and decided then and there that I'd make the best of this opportunity!

"When I told Jake back at bar at Mr. Mike's, he said, 'I always suspected you could do more than dance but thought you'd be a first-class gigolo before you'd be an honor student.' Of course, he finished by smacking me, like always.

"For the first time, I found school interesting, and I began to wonder what else I might want to try. I even found myself bringing some of the new material into my conversations at the club. Naturally, Jake warned me, saying, 'A dim bulb goes unnoticed in the club's lighting.'

"I could always count on him for a shot of wisdom.

"Waking for school was a challenge along with trying to be a regular teenager, but I pulled it off. Somehow I managed to pass classes, make it to some school dances, and even participate in a few extracurricular activities. I was good at art and was recruited to paint the sets for the school plays. It was fun. It was far from my mother's cancer, the bank, and even Mr. Mike's.

"One day in the middle of class, the phone rang. The call was about me participating in the school play! The teacher gave me a hall pass and said I was to report directly to the school auditorium and see the drama coach, Mr. Hague. I wondered if something had happened to the set I'd finished painting. I even wondered if he wanted me to take a small part in the school's upcoming production of *The King and I*. I wanted to try being on stage, but my nights were busy enough.

"I smiled to myself when I found out the reason I was sent for. It seems that the male lead in the school play, a member of the gymnastics team, could act, but dancing was not his thing! The most critical uplifting part of the musical is when the King of Siam takes Anna in his arms and dances around the stage to the song "Shall We Dance?" The answer to that most musical question was a resounding no! The king could not dance!

"After a brief introduction, the king and I were left alone in the auditorium with the music playing on a loop in the background.

"'It's like this, Richard,' I said to him. 'It's like taking a few different gymnastic moves and tying them together to make one elegant routine. Just take what you know about floor exercises and—'

"'What the hell do you know about gymnastics?' he interrupted. 'You don't know anything! I'd rather quit than do this stupid dance. Why the hell did they call you? Don't think I'm going to embarrass myself in front of the entire school. It's not going to happen. I'm out of here!' he yelled, throwing his script on the floor.

"I turned toward his exit, took three long steps, threw myself into a handspring, followed by a forward flip, ending in a split with both arms held high. All to the beat of the music!

"I taught him how to do the dance. Little did I know that he'd turn out to be *the* Richard Gere, the famous actor who would make movies like *Chicago* and, of all things, *Shall We Dance?* Life is funny!

"It was a year of hard work, confusion, and scrambling, but I graduated from high school for the second time in 1967. It had been a year of discovery that included a new direction, enrolling in the local community college as an art major with a minor in education. It seemed a good fit. In some ways, I'd been teaching for years, and art came as naturally to me as dancing."

Quitting Mr. Mike's

"I needed more time to study, so I left the bank. Leaving the routine of numbers and balances was easier than thinking about leaving Mr. Mike's, but by the end of my sophomore year, even Mr. Mike's had to go.

"I stayed late at Mr. Mike's, waiting for an appropriate time to tell Mike I was thinking about leaving. While waiting for Mike to finish talking to some guy near the front door, I looked over the place I'd come to think of as a second home. I loved the smells that drifted out of the kitchen, the music from the stage, and the memories of so many dance partners.

"I got lost in the past and was surprised when Mike broke the spell and spoke, 'Jake says you wanted to see me. What's going on? Your mom's okay? You need money?'

"'No, everything's fine, but—'

"'Spit it out, kid. I can't help if I don't know the problem. You didn't get one of these dames in trouble, did you?'

"'No! Nothing like that! It's just I have to stop dancing here.'

"'Why? You got a broken leg?'

"'No!'

"'You want one?'

"'What?'

"'That was a joke, kid. Now what's this all about?'

"'I need more time for school. I need the grades to get a scholarship. I appreciate everything you've done for me, and I love it here, but I think I've got to move on.'

"Once I finally said it out loud, I felt like I'd declared my independence and already made the decision to go.

"Mike put his hand on my shoulder and looked at me as if he hadn't really seen me for a long time and said, 'You're taller than I remember. When the hell did that happen?'

"Then as the idea of me leaving settled in, he began to strategize a way to keep me on the payroll. He was all over the place. He even implied that my exit from the dance floor could be part of a better plan, suggesting that bigger things might be right down the hall.

"I saw Jake raise an eyebrow when hearing this as he washed and stacked glasses at the bar. He intruded into the conversation by saying, 'Bigger isn't always better,' followed by, 'Size only counts if you have no finesse.'

"Mike was not amused and shot Jake a narrow-eyed look, saying, 'I was under the impression that you were hired as a bartender.'

"I tried to cover the situation with a little humor by asking Jake if he was 'speaking from personal experience.'

"Mike laughed, but I could tell he was irritated.

"'I'll miss seeing you out on that dance floor, kid,' Mike said, 'but maybe it's time for you to move along. We'll keep in contact. The door to Mr. Mike's is always open to you.

"'You know, maybe it's not the dancing thing but something else at Mr. Mike's that you might find interesting. Or you could go. Staying in one place for too long can be dangerous!

"'Keep moving! If you're not interested in moving up, move out!

"'If you're interested in moving up, just let me know!'

"Jake dropped a glass when he heard Mike talk about moving up. It shattered against the edge of the bar, sending pieces scattering in all directions.

"'That comes out of your salary, butterfingers,' Mike said with a smile but meaning it.

"'Sorry! That glass had a mind of its own. I caught it twice on its way down, but it was determined to slip through my fingers. You know what they say about things in motion and how they tend to keep in motion,' he added.

"Then Jake walked around the bar to where Mike and I were standing. He spoke directly to me with full concern and without jokes. In all the time I'd been at Mr. Mike's, I'd never seen Jake anyplace but behind the bar and never heard him interfere with Mike's business.

"'Did I overhear that you're in motion, Dancing Dave?'

"'I'm thinking about it, Jake. Thinking about moving on!'

"'There's somebody waiting for you at the bar, Jake,' Mike said as if it was an order.

"Jake faced Mike directly and spoke with an authority I'd never heard from him, 'He's young, Mike. Moving could be the right thing.'

"'You might be right, Jake. It's hard to hit a moving target,' Mike said and laughed out loud.

"'If it was easy, I'd have caught that glass,' Jake said quietly as he slowly walked back to the bar.

"I continued to take my serious dates to the club when I wanted to make a good impression. Mr. Mike would pick up the tab if he liked her looks. He usually did! One night while with a particularly pretty blond, I watched the new guy dance with a woman in a red dress. I wanted to tell him that he was holding her a little too close and that the job required a high level of sensitivity to personal space, particularly when interested parties were watching! He wasn't there long. Poor guy! My mother could have taught him that the dance wasn't about him at all.

"This was the night that my date suggested we go to another place in North Syracuse. It wasn't a swanky place, but it did have a live band that catered to younger people's tastes. I told Jake where we were going as I passed the bar on our way out of Mr. Mike's.

"The club was hopping when we arrived. The music was loud and dance floor crowded. There was an inviting upbeat energy in the air. Pitchers of beer were on every table, surrounded by laughing groups of young people who probably thought that we were overdressed for this club scene.

"This was a far cry from Mr. Mike's, but I could see its appeal. It was loose and casual, and I felt completely out of place. I asked my date to dance in an attempt to find something that seemed familiar.

"A couple of minutes into the dance, I was tapped on the shoulder by a guy dressed in a black suit. I thought that he might be cutting in, but when I turned to him, he said, 'Mike says to get out of here now!'

"'Why? We just got here.'

"'And now you're just leaving,' he shot back. 'Mike says you are to leave immediately and not ask questions.'

"'But—'

"'But nothing! Mike said you must trust him.'

"My date didn't like it, but we left without finishing the dance.

"The black suit followed us out the door and to my car and then waited for us to drive off the lot. As we did, I could see him run to a black sedan and then bolt away in the opposite direction, tires screeching.

"'Why'd you let him order you around like that?' she questioned. 'I wanted to dance.'

"'Who was he anyway? Who is Mike?'

"'I don't know that guy, but I know Mike, and I trust him. I don't know anything more than that. Sorry about the dance.'

"'Don't be sorry and don't call me again. I don't under-stand, and I don't want to. I won't go out with a guy who lets other guys push him around.'

"I took her to her apartment and then drove slowly past Mr. Mike's. I thought about going in but drove home for a restless night's sleep.

"The next morning, I read in the paper that the place where we had been dancing was firebombed. Nothing was left of it!

"I had lots of questions and wanted to ask Jake about the man in the black suit. When I approached the bar, Jake silently put the index finger of his left hand to his lips and shook his head no before pointing down the hall to the office door where muffled yelling could be heard. Then he whis-pered, 'You don't want to know.'

"I never did get my questions answered but kept stop-ping in periodically just because. Old habits are hard to break!

"I'm not sure whether Mr. Mike's was changing or me, but things seemed different, especially from the outside look-ing in. There were new faces among the regular crowd and activities that I didn't understand. Mike would disappear into his office with these guys for long periods of time. When he'd return to the main room, he'd walk directly to the bar and down a couple of shots.

"Once, when passing his office, I heard shouts and the sound of a bookshelf being pushed over. I wanted to go in, but Mike had warned me to never open his office door. I lin-gered for a few minutes, pretending to straighten a painting that hung on the wall outside his office. I heard somebody say, 'Listen, Mike, play by the new rules, or you won't be playing at all!'

"When the strangers left, I followed Mike to the bar where he sat, nervously watching the door. For the first time,

I saw Mike's hands shake as he put his signature silver lighter to the tip of his cigar.

"'Hey, kid,' he said, throwing a shot down before continuing. 'You were right! This isn't the best place for you hang out anymore. Go! Try something new. Get out of here. Find some young people. Buy a pair of blue jeans for God's sake. I don't know if I ever saw you without a tie. You got a plan?'

"'I'm working on it, Mike. I applied for a couple of scholarships, and I'm waiting for a response. How about you?'

"'How about me what?' he questioned, lowering his chin to look over his glasses.

"'Bob Dylan sings "The Times They Are a-Changin." Do you have a plan?'

"Mike looked at me in surprise and laughed out loud, saying, 'You don't miss a trick, do you?'

"'It's your fault! You taught me to be on the lookout, checking the room for signals and signs of change. You told me this place had its own climate and that I needed to be aware of the weather at all times.'

"'And what's your forecast?'

"'I'm seeing storm clouds on the horizon, Mike.'

"'I could have used a bright mind like yours on my team years ago.'

"'I've always been on your team.'

"Mike looked at me strangely for a long moment as if he was seeing me as his own son and gave me a bear hug, which lasted until Jake yelled, 'If the two of you are going to dance, I'll put on some music.'

"'I thought you liked your job,' Mike said as he pulled away. 'You look good, kid! Keep me posted on that scholarship business,' Mike said, slapping my shoulder as he walked away in a cloud of blue smoke. 'Don't worry about me. I can weather any storm.'

"I thought a lot about what Mike had said regarding being in one place for too long. I knew he was right, and my guts were telling me that the club wasn't what it once was and neither was I. There wasn't much that was new in my life, and I felt bored. I was doing the same things with the same people, going to the same places, and eating the same food. Sometimes I found myself laughing at the same old jokes, not because they were funny but because it was expected. It was just what one would do in a well-rehearsed routine. I needed some new moves.

"I had stayed in Syracuse for a thousand reasons but mostly because of my mother. She had been dying for years, dancing with cancer who was a cannibal with a huge appetite, biting off chunks of her, licking at the wounds, salivating for more. I thought her battle was my battle and stayed to guard the door.

"I might have stayed forever, but a letter arrived with news of a scholarship to a college in Kansas. It was the third scholarship I'd been offered, and this college was the farthest away. I told my mother that the pictures of the campus looked like a place where Mickey Rooney and Judy Garland would have gone and that I wanted to go there too. She said to go, adding that I couldn't cut in on her current partner while she was in the middle of teaching him a thing or two."

WALKING ON THE MOON

I almost forgot that Gordon was my invisible passenger and just continued the stories, if only to keep me awake.

"It was June, and I had the entire summer in front of me before leaving for Kansas. It was the summer of 1969, the summer of love, the summer that man walked on the moon! I spent that summer feeling that I was on a different launching pad, waiting for liftoff, waiting for that 'One giant leap!'

"A girl I knew from high school invited me to a big party celebrating the moon landing. She was a couple of years younger than me, which was a challenge after dating older women. She was playful and uncomplicated—no ex-husbands, no children, no baggage. I didn't know how to be with someone nearer to my own age but accepted the invitation. I needed to learn how to be with young people before heading to college.

"The owners of the party house were on vacation, and their daughter had organized a Moon Walk Blast as she called it. Everybody parked a distance from the house to hide the party from the neighbors. The young guests walked through the woods in the rear of the development and entered through the back door, carrying bags of snacks along with beer and wine and anything else they needed for the weekend.

"The television in the living room was tuned to the momentous event while the stereo in the basement blasted The Stone's latest release. There were about twenty people scattered throughout the house, including the bedrooms. Empty bottles were piled up in corners, and the air was thick with all kinds of smoke.

"I tried getting into the party mode, but it wasn't working for me. I wanted to bag the whole thing and swing by Mike's where I knew who I was and what to do. The only reason I stayed was because I didn't want to be rude to the girl who'd invited me. It was a long night!

"Around eleven o'clock the next morning, I wandered into the kitchen to get a handful of pretzels and a drink of water. I was feeling as out of place as I'd ever been. I felt old and distant from everything that was happening around me. I just couldn't make a connection.

"While at the sink, staring out the window, I saw what I assumed were the house owners pull into the driveway. I felt like the babysitter who'd let the juveniles go crazy in the parent's absence.

"I yelled the alarm before the car had even stopped and began pushing people and incriminating evidence out doors and windows. The girl who had invited me stuck by my side as the others fled with bags of bottles, chips, and clothes.

"At the last moment, one naked guy ran past us and out the back door. The parents had opened the trunk and were hauling out suitcases while I sprinted through the house, shoving everything I could find into trash bags to be hidden in the woods.

"My date caught the spirit of the moment. She pulled up bedspreads, turned off music, and flushed God knows what down toilets.

"I attempted to poorly start a fire in the fireplace to mask the lingering smell of suspicious smoke.

"I didn't know the parents, but to give their pan-ic-stricken daughter and my date time to take care of details, I walked out the front door to greet and delay them. I played the grown-up. It was easy. It was the first time I'd felt com-fortable in hours.

"I introduced myself and told them my girlfriend had stayed overnight with their daughter. I said they called me this morning after filling the house with smoke while trying to use the fireplace.

"The whole bit about using the fireplace slipped out before I could think. It was nearly ninety degrees! I kept going with a barrage of words, hoping they wouldn't have time to analyze the situation.

"'Don't worry,' I said. 'They just forgot to open the flu. It's a little smoky in there. I opened the windows a few min-utes ago when I arrived. You might want to hang out here for a bit till the air clears. How was your vacation? Where'd you go? You have a lovely home!'

"We stood there talking for a long time before the girls joined us, signaling that the house was ready.

"'Where's your car, son?' the father asked, and immedi-ately, I responded, drawing upon my years of making it up as I went along. I felt like the character Eddie Haskell from the old *Leave It to Beaver* television show from the late fifties. Eddie was always quick with the lie, ready to bamboozle and prepared to deflect responsibility! I thought the jig might be up but continued the smoke screen with confidence.

"'When the girls called, they neglected detailed direc-tions,' I said because it was the first thing that popped into my mind. 'I parked up the street and just walked around till I spotted smoke coming out the windows of this house.'

"None of this really made sense, but just like Mike told me, people believe what they want to believe. We pulled it off with a lot of lies and a lot of luck. It killed me when the parents thanked me for my help.

"By the time I got in the car and drove away, I wanted to keep going all the way to the middle of the country. I was tired of the lies, tired of myself. I wanted to start over again in a brand-new place and find a brand-new me. Even the lies at Mr. Mike's were easier to live with than the pretense of just being one of the kids. I wasn't a kid and really never had been."

IN THE NAVY

"At the time you were wishing for a brand-new start, David, I was talking to a Navy recruiter and getting an earful of sales pitch and information about traveling the world. I was intrigued with the military benefits program that included free—or near-free—education, health-care, housing, and enlistment bonuses. It all sounded good to me.

"I'd spent my college money and could barely put gas in my car. I wanted out of Texas and away from home. The idea of travel excited me, and I was ready for all kinds of changes!

"The recruiter also shared the disadvantages of military life, like spending months away from loved ones. I smiled when he said that because I saw that aspect of the Navy in a different way.

"The recruiter reviewed the military risks and fact that I could be at sea for extended periods of time. Then he asked if I was subject to seasickness. I said no, but in reality, I had no idea. He also asked if I could swim to which I proudly answered, 'Like a fish! Our school has a pool.'

"'Good,' he replied. 'Much of your basic training will be around and in the water.'

"What I didn't realize was the difference between swimming the calm waters of a heated pool and swimming in the freezing ocean while being pounded by six-foot waves!

"'There'll be lots of push-ups, pull-ups, sit-ups, and running,' he cautioned, adding, 'once you pass the Navy Physical Readiness Test, there will be rigorous classroom studies.'

"All of this sounded like a piece of cake, and as soon as I graduated, I signed up and was on my way.

"My mother cried when I said goodbye, and I felt guilty for not having a single tear of my own. All I kept thinking was that I was finally going someplace!

"In my entire life, I never threw up so much as I did in those first three weeks!"

GOODBYE, SYRACUSE

"I had completed two years at the community college, and now it was time to accept that scholarship.

"My mother encouraged me to go, saying, 'I'll be fine. This is your chance. Don't let it slip away! Go! Finish your bachelor's degree at the College of Emporia in Kansas. Say hello to Dorothy and the Tin Man for me! Home will be ready for you when you're ready for home.'

"On the nineteenth of August, 1969, I said my good-byes and began the road trip to Kansas. The car was over-loaded but ready for the open road. Beyond the mountains of western Pennsylvania, the world opened up.

"Flatland and a vast sky stretched wide from horizon to horizon filled with sun. I felt like I could breathe a deeper breath than I'd ever taken. I remember standing next to my car at a rest stop surrounded by thousands of acres of wheat fields. It was so quiet. I swear I could hear the blood pumping through my veins.

"I looked out at the distant four lanes of highway, busy with people traveling in both directions and realized I was one of them. I was finally going someplace.

"While stopping for gas in Ohio, I opened the trunk of my car, pulled out half my shit, and threw it in a dump-ster: button-down shirts, dress pants, polished black shoes, three good suits, and two huge boxes that I didn't even look through. I didn't care. Suddenly, it wasn't about what I was bringing but what I was leaving behind that mattered.

"I pulled off my shirt, jumped behind the wheel, and tore out of the rest stop in a squeal of burning rubber and cloud of blue smoke. Janis Joplin's 'Ball and Chain' blasted from my eight-track player and hot dry wind whistled through the open windows. There was nothing but road in front of me. I felt alive and thought that maybe, without the tight little world I'd built, I could be free to be young.

"At a little diner in Indiana where I stopped to grab lunch, a cute waitress started a conversation while warming my coffee as I stared at a map of the country.

"'Where're you from? You don't sound like you're from around here. Where're you headed?'

"I didn't answer right away! I was distracted by my reflection in a mirror across the counter. It scared me! I hadn't realized the long-term effect of being the good boy, following the rules and all that.

"Right then and there, I determined to make everything new, including me. I wanted to change that reflection!

"There was no Mr. Mike's and red dresses, no bank or secretary, no more keeping secrets, no more lies, no more nights at my mother's bedside. No part of me had to be the old me, unless I wanted it. I was free to discover whatever I could become.

"Driving across the country was giving me a brand-new perspective. From a little dot on the map, I saw the whole world as a huge dance floor, and it was mine!

"'I'm from New York,' I finally answered while running my fingers through my hair, pulling it lose from its slicked-back confines. 'I've never been around here before. I'm on my way to Kansas. After that, who knows?'

"The words sounded like the first really honest thing I'd said since I was a kid. I was free!"

THE COLLEGE
OF EMPORIA

The next two years were completely influenced by this new point of view. Nothing had to be restrained, hemmed in, sacrificed, or even lied about for appearances' sake. My hair was not groomed, and my suit was replaced by cutoffs and a T-shirt. I lost my sensitivity to personal space and completely embraced full-body contact.

I worked hard, made great friends, was on the dean's honor roll, participated in all kinds of activities, and loved every remarkable minute. I felt like I was catching up on a lifetime of things that had been put on hold and was grateful for this opportunity.

Living in a dorm was one of the best experiences of my life. Room doors were rarely closed, and small gatherings happened spontaneously and at all times of the day or night. After so many years of relative solitude, I suddenly had a close-knit family of friends and benefited greatly from the male bonding and mutual cooperation that was shared.

We laughed together, cried together, studied together, and dreamed together. I learned more in the dorm than I did in any class I ever took. Each person had something to teach me, and I was an eager student.

Every break would be filled with a trip in a different direction. I never sat still for too long and was always up for an adventure. All roads were new to me, so every turn was met with excitement, presenting fresh possibilities and forcing my world to grow larger and larger.

On Friday nights, the guys from my dorm hung out at a great little bar called The Fireside Lounge where we'd drink 2.0 beer by the pitcher, listen to the jukebox blare out the top-twenty hits, and talk about what was happening at Kent State and other war protests. When Simon and Garfunkel's rendition of "Bridge over Troubled Water" played, the place went quiet. We all knew that it could be us on the frontline in that faraway jungle. This reality bonded us together and made peace our common goal until the government used the draft-lottery system to divide us into three different camps.

According to your birth date, healthy young men would be in the following categories: those who would never be drafted, those who might be drafted, and those who would be drafted. This skillful political act reduced the number of war protesters and broke the bond that held us together like brothers. After that, the majority of the guys at the Fireplace lounge partied right through songs of peace.

The summer after my junior year was difficult. I went home where I'd secured a job and tried very hard to fit into the shoes, clothes, and community I'd left behind. It didn't work. I had become someone else, and there was no going home again. I tried to make the best of it and concentrated on earning enough money to return to Kansas for my final year. I was missing the camaraderie of dorm life that was waiting for me back in Kansas and missing many of my Syracuse friends who were in Vietnam.

I needed someone to talk to. I tried talking to my father about the war, but we saw it from totally different perspectives. I even got all dressed up and stopped in at Mr. Mike's, hoping to find some sense of belonging. Mr. Mike's had always been my sanctuary, but it had changed too. I stood exactly where I stood, the very first time I'd faked my way into the place. I leaned against the wall near the restroom where I had met Mr. Mike for the first time. It all seemed like a movie to me, a movie in which I had not been cast, and one which was not going to have a long run in the theaters. I left without saying a word to anyone.

The long and lonesome summer finally ended, and I packed up my car to head west. Upon arriving in Emporia, I soon discovered changes happened there as well. Some guys in the dorm had flunked out, some had transferred to other colleges, some had joined the service, and some just seemed to have disappeared.

There were new faces, too, but I was looking for ones I'd shared adventures with and had grown with. Some of those guys were still there, but life had impacted their thoughts, their direction, their perspective, and their plans, just like it had my own.

I began to realize that change is always inevitable, often unpredictable and sometimes necessary. I also began to understand that there are times when you must let go of the past to embrace the future.

In the beginning of my senior year, I met Terry. She was an incoming freshman and an art major. We clicked from the very beginning, and it scared me. I had just discovered freedom, and despite being drawn to her, I was afraid of what I felt. It had taken me a long time to find myself, and I worried about doing or saying anything that would jeopardize my liberation.

There was a constant push and pull going on inside me, wanting her and resisting her at the same time, like wanting to grow up and to stay young simultaneously.

One spring night, Terry and I met in front of Anderson Memorial Library and decided to go to the local drive-through that sold cheap wine, low-alcohol beer, and snacks.

I thought about Jake as we picked up the wine, paper cups, and a bag of popcorn. How he would have laughed.

We drove to Peter Pan Park, which made me smile. I kept thinking how appropriately named a place for me to be! We carried our purchases and blanket past the statue of William Allen White, who once said, "I am not afraid of tomorrow, for I have seen yesterday and love today."

We spread our blanket out in an open field where the star-spangled Kansas sky unfolded its startling beauty. We stared up in silence for the longest time, and when we did speak, it was in whispers, like we were in church. There was a warm gentle breeze blowing though the grass, soothing and natural as the words that we exchanged.

She was the oldest of eight kids and was more than ready to get out of the house and make a new life for herself in Kansas. She also had to be the grown-up way too soon.

I confessed that I never in a million years would have thought of Kansas as the place I'd grow to love, but I did. It was rich soil for my self-determination. That was the end of our philosophizing.

We sipped wine and kissed and kissed again, those full lips pressing against mine. That's when I knew I had to be careful. That's when I reluctantly reminded her of the curfew at the girls' dorm, folded up the blanket, and drove her back. It wasn't what I wanted to do. It was what I had to do. She was brand new, untouched, and vulnerable. I did not know how to be with someone like this, but I wanted to know.

College deferments ended during my senior year, and one by one, my dorm buddies were drafted. I also received notice that I was to report to an office in Kansas City for my Army physical.

The night before catching the train to comply with the dreaded orders, Terry and I gathered with a group of friends to listen to a recording of a live performance of Jesus Christ Superstar. It was performed by the original cast that was currently on Broadway. The rock musical was sung through with no spoken words at all. When the song "Heaven on their Minds" was sung, predicting coming calamity and death, the entire group had their hankies out. We all felt a strong correlation between the truth that was being denied in the lyrics and the truth being denied in Washington in regards to the war.

I managed to stay a civilian long enough to graduate with honors. My parents and youngest sister drove out for the ceremonies and saw me receive my degree. They had never been to Kansas before and never witnessed a college graduation. As a graduation gift, they gave me two used tires for my aging car. I was grateful but hoped it'd be something more meaningful than practical.

Following the event, they helped me pack up my dorm room and cram everything into my car for the trip home. After the last load was carried down, I lied, saying I'd forgotten something and sprinted back, taking the stairs, remembering each turn at every floor and all the things I'd loved about that old building and the people it housed.

I went into my empty room, stripped of the many crazy things that had been tacked up to make it mine. I ran my fingers over a dent in the plaster where, during my first semester, a baseball we'd been tossing ricocheted before it broke the window and fell four stories to the street.

I stood, quietly looking out through that repaired window, thinking how mended I'd become by encountering this place and wondered where I would land. I walked out of this epicenter of experiences and was turning the key in the lock for the last time when my mother's hand slid over mine, and we turned the key together.

She hugged me and said, "I can't tell you I know how this feels, but I can tell you that you can carry this pain. If there is ever a time you can't, I will carry it for you."

I've always believed those words were my real graduation present.

In the Army

"The next few months were spent waiting to be called to report for duty. I couldn't get a decent job because each interview started with a question about my draft status. The answer always knocked me out of the running.

"I ended up mowing lawns at a steel mill and drive-in theater. I liked the steel mill better. At the drive-in, the mower blades kept getting bound up by used condoms!

"On my birthday, Terry called from Kansas. She passed the phone around to a bunch of my friends. I could hear the party sounds and music playing. Each voice brought back memories. They all sounded so very young without the aging effects of waiting for the next shoe to drop.

"Terry said she loved me, just before hanging up.

"I was left in a very dark silence, remembering yesterday's goals of getting a teaching job, a master's degree, a new car, an apartment, a trip to Europe, a chance to make plans, and build a future of my own design. All those things had motivated me for years, and now, an external power was taking over the driver's seat, and I was back to being a passenger, not knowing where I was going or if I'd be coming back.

"Eventually, Uncle Sam caught up with me, gave me a buzz cut, uniform, and marching orders. Basic training started off with being told that we were now government property. A lot of guys in my platoon couldn't handle it. Somehow everything felt like familiar territory to me. There was a great need that couldn't be understood along with a lot of rules and a schedule that didn't include much sleep. I'd been there before! I missed the freedom, but at least I knew what freedom was and hoped that was what the guys in Vietnam were fighting for. I was still naive about such things!

"I didn't mind the food but hated the latrine where multiple toilets were lined up in an open space. Every grunt and fart reverberated for all ears and became fodder for impromptu humorous comments: 'Corn! I don't remember eating any corn.' 'If that splash down was yours, I can tell you right now there's not enough toilet paper in Louisiana for that job!' 'I haven't smelled anything that bad since that deer got run over by a tank and laid in the road for six weeks before they dragged it to the kitchen to make burgers.'

"There is no such thing as privacy in the Army, but you can get used to anything. Eventually, public bowel movements became as natural as washing one's hands at the sink. I was grateful for the dorm life I'd experienced in college that had prepared me for living with a bunch of men.

"I loved the marching drills. I found the rhythm of all those boots striking the ground in unison comforting. I liked the rows of synchronized swinging arms and the songs that accompanied the beat. I liked the crisp sharp turns and the commands that made everything happen.

"I didn't like the Army, but I understood it. I liked the fact that my father liked my being in the Army. I think he saw it as something we would have in common. Perhaps he was right, but it never would have happened if I had a higher number in the draft lottery. My number was eighteen, which meant I was going to get a uniform.

"I had marched in protest to the war when I was in college, but I had been raised to obey, and I did. I wasn't proud of that, but my father was. I owed him that!

"In basic training, I was called upon to be a squad leader, which put me in charge of a small group of men. I didn't feel the part, but since I always wanted to try acting, I threw myself into the role. I even had the costume! I took it all seriously, knowing the chances were good that Nam was in our future. I wanted to do everything possible to increase the likelihood of all of us coming home alive.

"Most of the guys were young and desperately afraid. Many of them had brothers or friends who were already there. They got letters from home filled with news of the dead, the dying, and the horrors of war. I tried to prop them up when they fell apart. I tried to build a team, a kind of family so they wouldn't feel alone in this madness. I acted myself into believing we were all going to make it and wasn't even nominated for an Oscar.

"After basic training, I went to AIT (Advanced Infantry Training). I was singled out for my marching ability and skill at taking and giving commands. I could sing out the cadence without hesitation and turn a hundred men on a dime. Why not? It was dancing! Chest out. Stomach in. Chin up! March!

"As platoon sergeant, sixty men were to be in my charge. The entire barrack was my responsibly. The first sergeant introduced me to the group as they stood in the yard at a sloppy imitation of attention. When the men were marched away to the mess hall, he took me to my quarters. It was a private room at the end of the second floor beyond the rows of bunk beds. Once the door to my room was closed, he gave me details about my orders and the men. He said that I'd be the second platoon sergeant to be assigned to this group.

"'What happened to the first one?' I asked, suggesting possible answers. 'Reassignment, deployment, emergency leave?'

"He looked over his shoulder to make sure the door was shut, saying in his slow Southern accent, 'He was murdered.

Somebody strangled him right there in the bed you're sitting on. It was done with a piece of piano wire. I don't know where they got it. I don't think there's a piano on the post.'

"'Murdered! What happened? Was there a court-martial?'

"'That's just it. You see, they never got the guy. They don't even know if it was just one guy. Oh, there were suspects and all, but with no witnesses and no hard evidence, the investigation fell flat. All they had was the body!'

"'What kind of guy was this former platoon sergeant?'

"'A complete bastard!' he said, lowering his voice. 'The men hated him. I didn't like him much either! He'd ride their asses about anything and everything. Each inspection was a nightmare! The more he pushed, the less they did, and the less they did, the more he pushed. It was an ugly cycle.'

"'I guess he pushed somebody over the edge.'

"'Pushed him all the way to hell! I expected this group to be busted up and sent to different forts all over the country, but here they are, and now they're yours!'

"'Why me? Isn't this a job for somebody with more experience, more stripes, more time in service?'

"'There's a war going on, my friend. All those guys are in Nam. I'm afraid your war is right here, and it starts right now!'

"He spent the next thirty minutes going over the roster and briefing me on each man. The roster read like a list of who's who among gangster wannabes. Many of them were in the military because a judge gave them this option, or jail. Their prior offences included everything from petty theft to attempted rape. There were notes regarding possession and selling of illegal substances, misdemeanors, public indecency, drunk and disorderly behavior, and every thug-related activity imaginable. And of course, there was the murder! Everyone on the base called this barrack the Last Chance Ranch.

"'I recommend locking yourself in at night, son,' he said as he stood and opened the door to exit. 'That door downstairs is required to be open but not yours. Remember we're scraping the bottom of the barrel these days. You never know who's creeping around after dark. Keep that duty roster up to date and maintain as much order as you can under the circumstances. If there are any problems, I mean like big problems, try to pull this fire alarm. It's right here at the top of the steps,' he said, tapping it twice as he started his descent. 'Lots of people come for a fire.'

"After I heard his boots echo down the stairwell and out the door, I walked back to my room. This time, I saw it as a crime scene. I didn't know if it was the crime that happened or one that might happen. I only had a few more minutes before the men were marched back and left in my charge. I was trying to think of ways of surviving this war I'd inherited and knew I had to make every action count. I grabbed my duffel bag and walked around the second floor, looking at the two rows of double bunks, reading the name cards out loud, 'Riccobinni, Harris, Savage, Nemire, Meyers, Gronski, Vesley.'

"There was one upper bunk without a second name card. I quickly checked the roster to verify that it was empty and claimed it for my own. As I heard the orders being issued to halt the group and bring them to attention, I wrote my last name on the card and left to take command of my men.

"It was the top bunk closest to the private room that would have been mine and not far from the fire alarm. No way was I going to close my eyes in a dead man's bed in a dead man's room. If I was going to die, it was going to be in front of as many witnesses as possible with bells ringing.

"The men were given orders to return to the barrack and prepare for inspection. Each one stood at attention at the foot of their bunk as I went one soldier at a time, trying to memorize every face and name. I manufactured an expressionless military posture and worked my way through the group.

"I didn't call anyone out for infractions of which there were many. I didn't think it was healthy. I kept thinking, *One step at a time*. My first step was to make it through the night.

"'Sergeant Page,' Vesley asked as I was about to dismiss the men.

"'Yes, Vesley. What is it?'

"'We noticed you took one of the bunks out on the floor, and we're wondering why.'

"I suspected this question might come up but didn't think it was going to happen on the first day. I blurted out the first thing that came into my head rather than appearing to not have an answer at all.

"'Army regulation 302-4-A states that a platoon sergeant may choose between any appropriate available area in the barrack. I choose to have nothing better than what my men have. We're all in this together. Dismissed!'

"I was sure there was no Army regulation of that sort and bet they wouldn't check. I dismissed them before another question could be asked and immediately went about emptying my duffel and organizing everything in my footlocker.

"The men watched my every move, trying to figure me out, identify weaknesses, cracks in the mask, and areas of vulnerability. I could feel their eyes but didn't meet them. Instead, I went about my business, stripped naked, wrapped a towel around my waist, and went down to the latrine to shower. One by one, they joined me to take care of personal business before lights-out.

"Just past the locker room and hooks of hanging mops were rows of toilets along one wall, urinals against another, sinks along the third, and a huge open shower making up the fourth. Everything and everybody was exposed in the latrine, and anyone seeking privacy was interpreted as being less than a man. Nakedness was a great equalizer, and an Army latrine was built to reveal inhibitions. I lathered up and took a long time rinsing off before toweling down and putting on my Army-green boxers and undershirt.

"Once all the men were in their bunks, and lights-out had been called, I climbed up to my bunk and waited for sleep. I listened to the sounds of the barrack: the breathing, snoring, and occasional coughs. Just as I was about to close my eyes, someone somewhere halfway down the row of bunks opposite me called out, 'See you on the range tomorrow, sergeant college boy!' I pretended I was asleep, but sleep wasn't going to happen.

"They'd gone through my trunk, read letters, and discovered I went to college. That was far from the street smarts they respected. They'd found something and interpreted it as weakness. I had to prove them wrong but didn't know how or when.

"The next five days were hell. No order was given without pushback, my bunk was torn up twice a day, and most of my personal belongings were stolen. The men faked obeying marching commands when any officer or the first sergeant was around and then became as rowdy as a street gang in their absence. They were trying to break me and were just waiting for me to report to the officer in charge. Every night, someone called out another message in the dark, 'Had enough, college boy? What're those books doing for you now? You're looking tired, buddy.'

"I was tired. The sleep I did get was nightmare filled and seldom. Sometimes I'd wake, heart pounding with my pillow soaked in sweat, sheet and blanket knotted around me by my twisting in the night. I'd lay there for hours, thinking, praying for an opportunity to turn things around before it was too late. I even wondered what my father would do.

"The fifth night into my new assignment, I woke but not from a dream. In the stillness of the dark room, I searched the silence for whatever could have pulled me from the depths of my exhaustion. There was nothing, and there was still nothing and then I heard it and heard it again.

"Someone was downstairs in the locker room. It wasn't the familiar midnight sound of the toilet but something else, something metal, perhaps locks being tampered with, pulled open, pried apart.

"I raised my head so no sound would be muffled by bedclothes and listened harder. There it was again and again. I rose to a sitting position and turned my head toward the stairwell, trying to focus on the dim red exit light at the top of the steps and the sounds making their way across the floor, ordering me to act.

"I swung my knees and legs over the edge of my bunk and slowly lowered myself, letting my bare feet touch the cold floor. As I walked toward the top of the steps, I looked back and saw that I was not the only one awake. I could make out the silhouettes of at least six other figures, propped up on elbows, angled in my direction. None of them moved.

"I crept slowly to the first floor and then down the steps and into the bright lights of the locker room and latrine. There in front of a locker wearing fatigues was the intruder hard at work, forcing a door open with the end of a mop handle.

"'Forget the combination, pal?' I shouted, the sound echoing around the room, bouncing off hard white porcelain across the tile floor and up the stairs.

"Startled, he jumped back, snapped the mop handle over his knee, and came at me with the jagged end.

"Jumping to the side, my bare feet slipped on the freshly mopped tiles, and I skidded to the floor, slamming my head against a urinal. He raised the weapon over his shoulder, like a left-handed batter and swung. I ducked, and the bat cracked in half on the porcelain, inches above my head, one end ricocheting into the dented mop buckets that rolled awkwardly across the tiles.

"He threw the other half at me, javelin style, but missed as I scrambled to my feet. Dizzy from the blow to my head, I lunged at him, throwing my left arm around his neck and pounding his face with three consecutive punches before he slipped away. All the while, I was yelling insults and accusations at the top of my lungs, trying to intimidate my assailant but mostly intended to bring my men running.

"As he landed a solid punch to the left side of my face, I saw the men steaming into the latrine but not to help, to watch! They circled us, lining the room, shoulder to shoulder, arms outstretched, pushing us back into the ring after each blow.

"I tried calling out their names in hopes that someone would stand with me, 'Vesley! Harris! Riccobinni!' No one broke rank. In the blur of blood and chaos as I twisted around and around, my mind snapped back and forth between that latrine and being at a dance in high school surrounded by cheering fans, calling out, 'Dancing boy.' I tried again, 'Gronski! Meyers! Nemire!' Nothing! Now I knew the rules of the game and gave up on the men as they chanted, 'College boy! College boy! College boy!' Just as Harris yelled, 'Where'd you learn to punch? Art class?' I reached beyond my main target and knocked Harris out cold, his head grazing the hot-water handle in the shower, steam filling the room. This overextension left me open for a slam to the gut, and my attacker let me have it with full force.

"I flew into the crowd and was flung back, off-balance and bleeding, on my knees, bent backward as he kicked me under my chin, sprawling me flat out across the floor. He stood over me, raising his leg, ready to stomp my face.

"Gathering all my strength, I reached up and grabbed his boot with both hands, twisting it almost in a circle. He screamed in pain and fell on his back where I straddled him, cupped both my hands together, and hammered his face right to left, then left to right and repeated again and again and again, blood pouring from his nose and eyes and ears until the military police pulled me off him.

"Three days later when I was released from the station hospital, I was ordered to testify at the military inquiry regarding the incident. I sat stiffly in my dress uniform due to three broken ribs and faced the officer's questions with two black eyes and a swollen lip. The military panel listened intently as I studied the room filled with members of my platoon.

"'Like I told you before, sir. I came upon the intruder breaking into the lockers, and he attacked me.'

"'And members of the Last Chance Ranch, what role did they play?'

"Again, I examined the audience, slowly looking each man in the eye before turning back to the officer and answering.

"'They saved me, sir! I don't know what would have happened if they hadn't done their duty.'

"'Are you sure that's the absolute truth?' he questioned with exasperation, knowing that it was not.

"'Positive, sir!'

"Three hours later, after some paperwork and another medical check, I returned to my barrack to find each soldier ready for inspection, except those who waited for me outside and held open the door. I dragged myself up the stairs, each man falling in behind me and gathering on the second floor.

"'Ready for inspection, sergeant,' Vesley shouted, and everyone snapped to attention, the heels of their polished boots clicking into place, like the gears of a well-oiled machine.

"'I recommend checking your area first,' he said, pointing over to my bunk and opened footlocker.

"I limped across the room, Vesley following me. My bunk was made-up, military tight, corners folded and creased, like they'd been ironed. In my well-ordered footlocker were all my missing items: the camera I'd bought at the PX, my transistor radio, letters from home, and something new. I pulled two full-color art books out and laid them on the bunk.

"'We stole them from the base library!' Riccobinni blurted out, Vesley rolling his eyes.

"'They're mine now,' I said, and they were, not just the books but the men! From that moment on, we were a team, and they chose me as their leader.

"That night, I lay wide-eyed in my bunk, thinking about my father and the team of men he was a part of in the Army. He was only seventeen when he enlisted. He must have grown up with those guys, many of whom he watched die. That bond held them close and held me distant. For the first time, I felt an inkling of what that bond must be like and understood its power."

"Did you stay in contact with any of those guys?" Gordon asked.

"No! I tried, but those that survived went back to their own world. I have thought about them many times over the years and am so grateful for what they taught me."

"Taught you? Lessons on how to get your head bashed in? What in hell did those hoodlums teach you?"

"They taught me to never give up and that there is more to me than what I knew."

"Did they teach you to watch your back and carry a knife?"

"No! They taught me how to understand my father."

THE DRILL SERGEANT'S ACADEMY

"After AIT, I was sent from the swamplands of Fort Polk, Louisiana, to the Drill Sergeant Academy at Fort Knox, Kentucky. My first sergeant, the one with the Southern accent, recommended me for the academy, saying, 'Who'd have guessed you'd turn around that disgrace of a platoon? Nothing but criminals! I'd have bet next year's cotton they'd kill you! The Army needs men that can make a silk purse out of a sow's ear.'

"The Drill Sergeant Academy was absolutely no joke. Everything had to be exactly to military standards. During inspections, you had to stand at the foot of your bunk at attention with your footlocker wide open. Your toothbrush had to be an inch from your toothpaste, which had to be an inch from your razor, which had to be an inch from your soap, which had to be an inch from your shampoo. The first sergeant carried a ruler, and he used it with surgical precision.

"There were standards for starching and folding uniforms, polishing boots, personal appearance, and everything else!

"Once, the first sergeant overhead one of the guys complaining that the next thing that was going to be regulated and measured was the length of your shit. He was ordered to

175

sit on the john until he made one exactly six inches long. He sat there for an entire Saturday.

"During AIT, we had to crawl on our stomach inches below multiple rounds of live ammunition, keeping our faces in the mud as we heard the zing of bullets grazing our helmets. Along with learning how to complete a mission while under fire, we learned how to take apart our M16 rifle, clean it, and reassemble the weapon in a matter of seconds. This also applied to machine guns and bazookas. Another timed military experience was the gas chamber where we were sent full pack and locked in as the gas was released. Our job was to retrieve our gas masks and put them on properly before we choked to death.

"Now at the academy, everything needed to be accomplished in half the time granted us during basic training, or AIT. There were also many written tests and constant pressure from the regular Army instructors whose job it was to break us! There was bullying, name-calling, intimidation, and constant ridicule to contend with.

"I understood that we were being trained for leadership positions on the ground in Vietnam and that they were trying to weed out those who might fail in the field. What rattled me the most was seeing some of the big tough guys crumble under the strain.

"This one guy from Iowa was six feet four inches tall and had an ego twice as large. He couldn't wait to get his stripes and was already attempting to bully other trainees. He thought he was a righteous, badass, and took every opportunity to have the sergeant in charge witness each browbeating move. The sergeants saw through his antics and crushed him with discipline and demands. I remember him breaking down and crying like a baby when he flunked out of the academy.

"I often wondered if the platoon sergeant that had been murdered in what was to be my bed had the same personality disorder.

"One morning, while in formation, readying ourselves for inspection, every siren, bell, and alarm filled the air with a deafening array of noise, and we were marched double time back to the barrack. The base was transformed into a mass of convoys and orderly blocks of marching men in full pack.

"At the barrack, we were told to pack everything into our duffel bag and return to formation in no more than ten minutes to receive our orders.

"Despite the continuing noise, rush, and chaotic nature of this break in our routine, the men were quiet. None of us needed to question or speak. We knew what was happening and where we were going!

"Once we were reassembled in the yard, the first lieutenant addressed the group.

"'When the trucks arrive, you will be taken to the base airport where you will board a military transport and receive further orders.'

"We were held at attention until the trucks arrived, so there were no conversations among the men, just one-word whispers. 'Vietnam!'

"At the base airport, we were re-formed into a long straight line and marched slowly to the transport. By this time, the screaming sirens, pounding bells, and beep, beep, beep of the alarms were overpowered by the roar of jet engines! I couldn't even hear myself think.

"One by one, I watched each soldier board the plane, allowing me to take one more step closer to a war I was trained for and a war I did not believe in.

"Suddenly, a military messenger interrupted the movement. The officer in charge was handed orders as I stood three soldiers back from the transport's ramp. Those three and I along with all those behind us were re-formed on the tarmac to salute as the transport pulled away and took flight, disappearing into the gray clouds.

"That night, alone in my bunk, I silently wept.

"'Did you ever end up going to Vietnam?' Gordon asked.

"'No, thank God! The war strategies were changing, and the number of troops was being drawn down. More air power was being deployed, meaning fewer boots on the ground.'

"Support for this military action was failing. The continuing protests had turned the tide, and Washington was finally responding!

"I was eventually transferred to reserve status and then sent home to a place I couldn't stay. I was filled with stories that I didn't know how to tell or who to tell them to. I couldn't find myself in this familiar setting. It was like being a little bit crazy, like trying to fit into sneakers I wore when I was twelve. Everything pinched! The love was still there, but I could not be!"

ROAD TRIP TO VIRGINIA BEACH

"In less than a month, I was packed for a trip. I was looking for something else, but I didn't know what it was. I just knew it wasn't going to be found in Syracuse. I jumped at the first chance to get away, which came sooner than I expected and yet not soon enough.

"I didn't even do any research, or make a list of possible destinations. I had a quick phone conversation with an old friend who I hadn't seen in years. He'd been struggling since returning from the war and was up for going anyplace. He suggested we go to Virginia Beach for a week or so. The next thing I knew, I was packed and on my way to pick him up.

"I kissed my mother goodbye. It was difficult, like all the goodbyes we ever shared. We always knew the current goodbye could be the last one, especially since the medicine that had been so successful at keeping her in remission was now unavailable.

"She had not been able to get her prescription filled and called the doctor who called the pharmaceutical company and was told that the drug worked on so few people that it was no longer financially profitable and was being discontinued.

"My father, along with the doctor, called all over the country and was able to purchase a substantial amount, but not enough.

"I had never connected the relationship between profit and medicine before and found it a hard pill to swallow.

"I pulled out of the driveway and headed up the street, anxious to be on the road.

"For the first time, I felt I was rehearsing for a more permanent goodbye to everything—the houses on my street, the school yard, the movie theater. I saw them all differently, in a way that highlighted their age and faults. I looked in the rearview mirror and had the profound realization that it was all soon to be behind me.

"The car window was down, but the summer breeze was unable to muss the results of my military experience. It crossed my mind how I lost my hair while others lost their limbs or their minds or their lives.

"On a whim, I pulled into Mr. Mike's parking lot, got out, and leaned against the car, blistering hot in the July sun. I had never been there in the daylight. It didn't look as classy as it did in the dark when I was fifteen. I was thinking about Mr. Mike's during its heyday and could almost hear the music playing when a somewhat-familiar face came out of the front door.

"'Hey!' he shouted while crossing the parking lot. 'Dancing Dave! Is that you?'

"'I'm surprised you recognized me,' I shouted back.

"'I didn't! I recognized your junk car. Where's your hair?'

"'Uncle Sam took it.'

"'You should have made him take your wheels instead. A woman might go out with a guy who looks nearly bald but never in a crate like this.'

"It was Jake, a little thinner and grayer but still the same funny bartender who had poured me a thousand ginger ales back in the day.

"We shook hands as he pointed up at the sign that read, 'Mr. Mike's.'

"'That's coming down tomorrow!' he said. 'It's going to be a beer joint! I don't know why I'm staying. Pizza!' he shouted. 'They're going to serve pizza! New owner, new name, new everything! They say they're going to strip the place bare and give it a whole new look: barn-board walls covered with wagon wheels and farm shit! Oh, yeah, fake beams in the ceiling too! No live music, no tablecloths, no fine dining! Pizza!' he repeated.

"'Dancing?' I questioned.

"'I haven't a clue, but if there's square dancing, I'll quit! I miss the good old days!'

"'Were they as good as I remember?'

"It took a while for Jake to respond. He pinched his eyes shut, forcing a cluster of wrinkles to betray his youthful spirit, looked back at the building, and then turned to me.

"'It was Camelot, my friend. Yes, it was Camelot! You remember. It was an upscale costume party on steroids. But it's gone now!'

"He shook his head as if to force old images from his mind and asked me what I'd been up to. I struggled to string the years of experiences together in a way that made any sense and then tried to bring the conversation back to common ground.

"Jake was lost in our shared yesterdays. He talked about women in red dresses, after-hours parties, and all the music that stopped when Mike was shot!

"'I was at Fort Knox when my mother sent me the clippings from the newspaper. I still don't know how she connected me with this place. Did they ever find out who did it?'

"'The police didn't have any answers, just questions that were ignored. There weren't any suspects, only a hundred witnesses who saw nothing, heard nothing, and would say nothing.'

"'I ran to Mike, but it was too late. It had been too late for a long time!

"'I took Mike's silver lighter from his hand, sliding it into my pocket as a keepsake. Then I sat on the dance floor, watching the tip of his cigar slowly turn to ash while waiting for the police.'

"'I remember lying on my bunk, reading his obituary over and over. It happened when I was in fatigues, preparing for the bombs and bullets of Vietnam, and he got shot in his best suit with music playing.'

"'Just different wars, my friend! You did the right thing—leaving when you did. It was never the same again.'

"'You never left, Jake. Why don't you leave now?'

"'It's too late for me. Besides, leaving takes courage, and I don't have much anymore.'

"'Maybe it takes courage to stay.'

"'There's the Dancing Dave I know, always seeing the very best in everybody. Now get the hell out of here. You're young! Go make a difference in this world!'

"We shook hands without any words, just a look that I can feel to this day. He slapped me on the side of the head and smiled.

"I got in the car and drove away without looking back. I could hear him yelling, "Run, boy! Run," the final words to his favorite Broadway musical.

"A half hour later, I picked up my high school friend who I'd only spent twenty minutes with since his return from Nam. I didn't realize until hours into the trip that I really didn't know the guy in the passenger seat anymore.

"He'd talk nonstop about what he'd seen in Vietnam, the babies he saw die, and the hookers he'd slept with. Then he'd doze off, giving me a few moments of peace before screaming himself awake from a Nam flashback that left him demanding we stop at a bar.

"What should have taken four hours took three stops and eight hours to get to Lansdale, Pennsylvania. That's where I left him at a local beer joint. I needed a break from his crazies, and I wanted to visit Terry, the girl I'd met in college.

"On the way to her parent's home, I kept hoping she hadn't changed!

"She hadn't changed, or if she did, it was only for the better. Her eyes still held that Kansas perspective I'd discovered out in the land of tall grass, rolling hills, and big sky. We hardly took breaths while trying to catch up on each other's lives. Then suddenly, it was time to kiss goodbye. It was a good kiss, tender and determined, sweet and sexy, proper and promising.

"I wanted a longer visit following that particular kiss, but she was leaving for her last year of college, and Virginia Beach was waiting for me.

"Terry reminded me of something precious I had lost and found again!

"'I'm only interested if someone lost their virginity,'" Gordon laughed, adding, "'and I don't think that can be found again.'

"'Don't be so sure. A lot of things can be stitched back together. Yes, modern medicine can be amazing! I know an older woman who used to dine at Mr. Mike's. She had a whole-body lift. She looked fantastic but moved to a different beat, and no surgery could tighten up her brain.'

"'The wear and tear of the passing years always leaves scars but rarely wisdom! Just look at me! I'm beat to shit and still haven't learned which way is up.'

"'Don't be so hard on yourself. You've learned plenty!'

"'Have I, David? I still have so many questions.'

"'The more you know, the more you realize what you don't know. It's like looking at the night sky. The more you look, the more stars you see.'

"'I've looked at some things pretty damned long and hard and still haven't gained an enlightened perspective.'

"'According to who?'

"'According to me! I might have looked at the stars too much and missed what was right in front of me.'

"'That sounds like an enlightened perspective to me!'"

GORDON'S WILLING PARTNER

"Once, during the first year that I was in the hospital, the doctors told me that I was still able to have children. I was shocked! I hadn't had an erection since before the accident. They said it could all be done by extracting my seed with a needle and planting my donation into a willing partner. That, along with some chemical fertilizer, could make the garden grow."

"Did you have a willing partner for this agricultural experience?"

"I did. My nurse and constant companion was positive we could make this work. I was the one who was not willing. I am the one who finally realized how unfair our relationship was to her. She wanted everything—the marriage, the house, the yard, and the kids! She was so very sure we could pull off the masquerade."

"What happened?"

"I couldn't let her be tied down to a half-baked version of a dream. I sent her away. I refused to see her. I gave her a chance to do it right."

"Was that right for you?"

"I haven't figured that out yet."

"In all these years, you never told me that story. Why now?"

"Running out of time, my friend, if not now, then when?"

"Do you want to talk about it?"

"No! It's too late. It's all too late! Life's sweet milk has been wrung out of yesterday, today's has gone sour, and tomorrow looks bone-dry!"

"Wow! You really know how to whip up a happy ending."

"I can't help it. The story ends where it ends, and that's where it ended!"

"That story didn't last longer than twenty miles. I suppose you think you've done your share of storytelling for the day. Well, forget that! You can start now by giving me the details of some great adventure and make it last for at least a hundred miles."

"I can't."

"What do you mean you can't? Tell me a damned story!"

"I wish I could, Dave. That was the last one that had to be told. I've searched my memory bank, and most of what's in there are stories I've read, or listened to on recordings. Then there are the millions of hours of television dramas and mysteries that are stored up here," he said while pointing to his head.

"The greatest adventure of my life has been the struggle to survive! It's the story of routines and regularity. It's a study in patience and boredom. It's the picture of hospital beds, oxygen tents, ambulance rides, and multiple emergencies. I haven't done much."

"What about your drawings?"

"Oh, I'm proud of them, but they're not originals. I redraw someone else's photographs. It's a tedious mechanical effort that fills my days, just like I fill in the blank spaces with lines and shades and textures, but it's not real. I am as boxed in and framed as my drawings—unable to move, change expression, live, and get knee-deep and dirty in the day.

"I'll tell you what I've got. I've got you, brother! I've got your authentic stories. I see things through your eyes, feel them through your fingertips. You take me with you where I can live beyond the wheelchair and hospital bed. I've always been thirsty for life. Your words quench my thirst!

"The more you live, the more I live. We're connected! I can't understand why you continue to visit after all these years. Is it pity? Do you have some false sense of responsibility to Sony and think you must take care of her invalid little brother? What do you get out of this?"

"I get to learn how to use a Hoyer lift for hauling your sorry ass in and out of bed. I get to empty your urine bag and smell piss regularly. I get to wipe drool and bits of tacos off your chin. I get to stretch my budget to include you in my world, hear your sarcasm, and periodic vulgar outbursts. I get you!"

"I'm sorry I asked!"

"Oh, but there's more! I also get to hear your opinions and perspective on politics, personalities, movies, books, news, and art. I get to engage in thoughtful conversation and hysterical laughter. I get to have different experiences and create new stories in which you play a leading role. I get to know the original and authentic Gordon and that's worth all the shit I have to put up with! Now what do you have to say to that?"

"If I tell you a story, will you shut up? I might have one more!"

"Okay, then! I knew you were holding out on me."

I Didn't Want
to Like You

"When Sony first called me to say that you were coming with her to California for a visit, I didn't know what to think! Her letters had been full of you and then you and Terry and then you and Terry and your sons. I felt like I knew you already and yet I wondered how it could be that all of you shared this remarkable and close relationship.

"She used to keep me up to date on your activities as much as she did on her own. I knew each theater production you were in and those that you wrote and directed.

"She'd send me copies of your published works along with articles and reviews.

"She also sent multiple postcards each time she traveled with you, your wife, and your kids.

"I was a bit jealous that she had your family until I finally realized that it also meant that I had all of you as well. It took me years to figure that out!

"When you walked in my door for the first time, standing so straight and tall, I was nervous and intimidated. I'll never forget what you did. You threw your arms around me with a big hug, saying, 'I've been waiting to do this for years!'

"I will tell you right now. Very few people hug a quad! They're afraid they will break a bone or get covered in drool, dislodge a tube, or catch something horrific!"

"Gordon, I remember that first meeting. You were cold and distant, like a Swiss mountain I once climbed!"

"Shut up! I'm telling this story. Enough of your metaphors! I wanted to cry! I wanted to scream! I wanted so badly to hate you!"

"I thought you did!"

"Then you threw me off track by talking about all the things my sister had kept you informed of over the years. I wasn't just a list of physical conditions, bedsores, and infections. You knew about my going to college and my drawings, interest in art history, and love of film.

"You didn't see me as a brainless fleshy lump attached to a chair. You joked with me and caught me off guard with your humor and strong opinions.

"Twenty minutes after you arrived, we were out on the deck, drinking a few beers while debating what films were going to be nominated for an Oscar. You even dared to disagree with me and we debated."

"We argued?"

"Yes, damn it. We argued and used some pretty strong language! I hadn't felt that alive in years!

"I wanted to hate you so much but then you suggested we all go out to dinner!

"You weren't afraid to be seen with me, eat with me, or even drive my access van. You never waited for me to say I needed my urine bag emptied. You just hopped up and wheeled me to a private place to make the magic happen."

"I have a history of being around people that need a little assistance."

"You didn't let me sit in a restaurant with crumbs on my face. You grabbed a napkin and wiped the mess away without batting an eye.

"While we talked, you raised a water glass so I could catch the end of the straw with my tongue, and you held the glass until I was done sipping.

"Before the meal, you cut up my meat, and after the meal, you checked me out, making sure nothing needed to be wiped up or dealt with before I exited the place.

"I really wanted to hate you, but you always kept coming back!

"Each of your visits have been filled with movies and dining and road trips and hours of conversation and your fucking stories that left me feeling whole.

"I tried to hate you, but I couldn't!

"Having a beautiful wife helped you too! I'm a quad, but I'm not dead!"

"I never wanted to like you either, and I still don't!"

Gordon called me a bastard, laughed, and yelled, "Your turn!"

"My turn to do what? Smack you?"

"You can't smack me. You can't abuse the disabled! You'll go to jail!"

"Might be worth it!"

BECOMING WRITERS

"Tell me about how you and Sony became writers."

"Well, in many ways, we were destined to write because we always told stories. Sony told you stories, and I told stories to my little sister. It's how we saw the world and how we passed the world we saw on to others.

"It didn't happen overnight. It was slow growth, through trial and error. We messed around with arranging and rearranging words until the words had a life of their own, and characters emerged right off the page to tell a story.

"Sony's big breakthrough came when Analogue Science Fiction Magazine published her short story, *Cyber-tone*. She was very excited and knew this was her first step into the professional writing world.

"Then came *Rockabye Baby*, my personal favorite, and then her first novel, *Red Genesis* in 1991, which she dedicated to your mother. She thanked both you and me in the opening of that book.

"Sony told me she considered you to be her first audience. I guess my telling you stories is a natural extension of an existing tradition.

"My own writing took a different path. I was more drawn to the stage, poetry, and lyrics. I self-published a book of poetry called *This Side of Dawn* in 1975 and started to make appearances at poetry readings, sharing original works and singing at coffee houses. Here and there, I'd get a poem published, but mostly, they were performed.

"Eventually, I started writing and sharing monologues, which led to being invited all over the country to teach other creative types at writer's conferences.

"I also began to write plays, like *Fire Escape Philosopher*, *September's People*, *In the Garden*, and many others. Most of my plays were produced in the Philly area, including *If I Knew Then*, which was produced at the Annenberg Theater.

"One of my favorite plays was called *Recipes*. This particular piece was produced at the Montgomery Theater and received a lot of attention. This led to my being contracted to write the musical *Resisting Gravity*.

"That resulted in an invitation to participate in the American Society of Composers, Authors, and Publishers in New York City. Things just grew from there."

"So why aren't you famous? What happened? Didn't you have the talent?"

"That's possible, but before I could find out, the stroke happened! Life happened!

"Remember, I was not alone on this journey. I had a wife and family. As soon as I started to recover, I needed to find a way to bring in a regular paycheck. I needed insurance. I needed security. I needed to get my priorities straight!

"I went back to teaching art! Don't think for a moment that this was some big letdown or sacrifice. I loved it! Other than parenting, there is no job more important than teaching!

"You'd be amazed how much my students helped me to recover. I love the classroom. Each opportunity to assist in a student's growth results in your own growth!

"When I got to the point where I could type, I began writing again. Eventually, I regained the stamina to be on stage and performed during the summer months and on weekends. I continued to do one-man shows but embraced the reality that was before me, even though my resolve was periodically tested.

"Once, I received a phone call from Germany. It was a friend of mine who I'd been on stage with and who knew my singing range and theatrical background. She was with a touring company whose lead-tenor had just walked out on them.

"She handed the phone to the director who offered me the opportunity take over the lead along with a one-year contract. I put him on hold for a minute to share the news with Terry. She said to take it, but my three little boys were standing there, and I knew where my duty was. I didn't go but always knew Terry would have supported any decision I'd made. This made it easier to stay, to teach, and to raise my sons.

"In time, I became the manager of professional development for the school district, teaching teachers how to teach. I became a principal and then the director of instruction for all eighteen schools in the district, kindergarten through twelfth grade.

"By that time, I was traveling around the country, speaking and performing at educational conferences. In many ways, I was on the stage again, just with a different audience."

"Didn't you miss the limelight?"

"Fame was never the goal. I had the experience of seeing my name and picture on billboards. I remember my oldest son pointing out the car window and shouting, 'Look, Dad, it's you up there.' When I sang and danced the lead in Toyland for Pennsylvania stage.

"That was great, but making a positive difference, being productive, being creative, being happy, and being with my wife and children, those were the goals. I've had a taste of fame. It was like dessert, but I wanted the entire meal!

"I've had the excitement of lots of opening nights, but my one true triumph is my family! That's what I'm really proud of!"

"You're serious, aren't you?"

"Yup!"

"And how about my sister? What was her triumph?"

"Building a successful teaching career and getting published meant everything to her!"

"Was there any rivalry between you?"

"We shared our successes! That's why we were friends. There was rarely any competition between us. We didn't do presentations together, but we supported each other's dreams."

"Did the two of you ever fight?"

"We had our disagreements and misunderstandings but found a way to talk things out. In fact, we were in the middle of one of those times of not seeing eye to eye when I had the stroke. She showed up at the hospital anyway, and life went on. Life is too short to waste time with anger or regrets. Friends don't have to walk in lockstep. They just have to respect each other's opinions."

"I fought with my sister once, and it was horrible!"

"What was the fight about?"

"It had to do with my nurse. Sony took her side and wanted me to have the wedding and the whole nine yards. Even when I shared my concerns regarding our family's genetic misfortune, she wanted me to take the chance, insisting I engage in explaining in detail every reason for my position. The argument did wonders for developing support for my point of view.

"She forced me to embrace a stronger defense as I articulated my deepest fears and reservations. The dispute became the rehearsal I needed before facing the woman who would not be my bride."

"Did you hold onto that anger?"

"No, I was grateful! The exchange prepared me for the real showdown. Without Sony, I could never have found the words. Finding the right words is essential to being understood. The right words along with the right tone, volume, and expression can make or break communication!"

"When you had that well-rehearsed conversation with your leading lady, how did it go?"

"She cried! I wasn't prepared for tears, only words. The tears were more powerful. I resorted back to what I'd learned as a kid. I got angry, insistent, arrogant, irrational, and nasty. Those were the elements of speech that drove her away."

"After the stroke, all essential elements of speech were beyond me. Even if I could find the right word, there was no guarantee I could say it. My friend Mary found that I did better by repeating one word over and over again as loud as possible so I could practice forcing a lot of air across my vocal cords.

"She had me stand out on the deck behind the house that looked out over a valley, choose a simple one-syllable word, and scream it at the top of my lungs.

"After repetitive shouts of dog, cat, roof, neat, swell, and other moronic outbursts, Mary, who is not known for being subtle, brought the lesson to a sudden stop."

"Wait a minute! This is boring as hell! Let's tie some emotion and meaning into this disaster! How do you feel?"

"Like shiout," I answered.

"Did you mean like shit?"

I shook my head yes.

"Oh, no, you slacker! Answer me with words, or I'll push you off the deck."

"Yeis, I fel lik shiit!" I screamed back.

195

"Great! Lean out over the railing and tell the world how you feel."

I grasped the railing and yelled, "I fel lik shiit!"

"Louder, and say it like you mean it, you bastard. I know you've got some anger in there. Let it out."

I took a big breath and yelled, "I fel like shiit!"

"Come on, you wimp. Put your balls into it."

I was getting angry and shouted again, only louder, "I feel like shit." And then repeated, "I feel like shit." And even louder, "I feel like fucking shit!"

Suddenly, from somewhere down in the valley, we heard a man's voice ring out, "Me too!"

"Mary and I laughed like hell."

"She sounds like quite a friend. Was a she friend of Sony's too?"

"Not at first! It took a while for that friendship to grow. Mary's not the type to give up easily! She persisted, and eventually, Sony came around. They used to go to the movies together until Sony was lost in the fog of dementia, and even then, Mary would visit her regularly.

"Mary was with Sony when she died in that facility where she felt so safe and comforted. I was giving a presentation at a conference near Niagara Falls and had asked Mary to look after your sister while I was gone. She passed away with a friend by her side. I'll always be grateful for that!"

"Was Mary a writer too?"

"That's how we met. I was one of the judges at the Philadelphia Writer's Conference, and Mary got second place in playwriting. We became friends and even did some writing and theater work together. Mary went on to develop a great reputation as the writer of a blog called Heartprints.

"Mary was my assistant for the production of my play, *Recipes*, and also for my musical, *Resisting Gravity*. One year after the stroke, while visiting Mary and her husband in Jakarta, she and I flew to Malaysia to present a five-day workshop in Kuala Lumpur. After that, we toured Indonesia, China, Korea, and Singapore."

"Was my sister resentful of Mary's relationship with you?"

"Sony was always leery of any woman who appeared to move too close to the center of my world."

"Were there many?"

"Yes! There were a lot. I have always had a great appreciation for women and welcomed their friendship."

"Did you welcome anything more?"

"I've spent much of my life on the road, performing, teaching, and lecturing. A man alone out there is presented with many opportunities. Lots of women are drawn to a guy who commands the stage, sings, and knows how to dance."

"You didn't answer the question. Little flings, extramarital affairs, sex on the side?"

"Nope! Not once in all those years. The chances were plentiful, but my heart wasn't into it."

"What about your dick?"

"I kept that out of it too. Terry is the only one for me. That's how it is. I would never mess that up!"

"Were there women who tried? Sony's letters mentioned lots of leading ladies over the years who seemed interested in a leading man."

"Some tried, and some tried harder than others! I set them straight. I made the rules! It was friendship or nothing. Some chose nothing."

"You're a better man than me!"

"No, I'm just a man who knows a good thing when he's got it!"

ISTANBUL

"Hey, Gordon! Wake up! Look at that sign on the side of the road! I've been seeing lots of them advertising some pretty cool shows in Las Vegas. Are you interested in a little side trip?"

"No. I've got to close my eyes for a while. I'm feeling a little weird.

"Besides, you have to get to the hospital, remember? The real me will be waking up soon. Talk to me while I rest."

"About what?"

"You've told me stories about Joshua, the train runner, and Michael, motorcycling in Crete. Tell me a story about traveling with Matthew. Take me on that trip with you."

I drove on, listening to Gordon's shallow breathing and deciding how to start the next story as his eyes slowly closed.

I said Gordon's name few times to make sure he was still with me. He didn't respond, but periodically, I heard a groan. I told the story anyway.

"Sony, Matt, and I flew to Istanbul from Greece as part of his grand tour experience when he was fourteen.

"This was the first time I'd ever been to this ancient place, and I was excited to visit the city they called the gateway to the east. It is the only city in the world that spans two continents, and from the moment we arrived, we were overwhelmed by the difference in architectural styles, food, and dress.

"We settled into a cheap hotel and immediately hit the streets with our city map and caught a bus to Hagia Sophia, the Byzantine masterpiece. We were inspired by this Grand Mosque, which was formerly the Church of Hagia Sophia. Its minarets were unlike anything we'd seen in Europe, and the call to worship brought thousands of people to their knees.

"Then we went to the famous Blue Mosque from the Ottoman era. It was built in the Islamic style and seemed almost otherworldly and powerful.

"Ancient cultural influences were everywhere including Roman, Egyptian, and Persian. It was the most international of all the cities I'd ever visited and made each of us feel as if we were in the middle of the crossroads of the world.

"We walked the streets for hours and ended up at the Topkapi Palace and Museum where the sacred relics, including the belongings of the prophet Mohammed, have been preserved for five hundred years.

"Among their treasures is an ancient map that no one could make sense of until a photograph was taken of the earth from space, showing in great detail shorelines of the Earth's continents. The mystery of how this map could have been drawn remains unsolved and fascinated Matthew.

"Later, we walked through the huge leather market and ate Manti, a dumpling filled with lamb, yogurt, and garlic.

"It was late by the time we returned to the hotel. Sony decided to stay in for the night, but Matt and I headed out to see the city after dark. As we were leaving the hotel, the manager suggested we put our passports and credit cards in the hotel safe and take only what we could afford to lose. We followed his suggestion and walked down by the water where cedar-clad buildings have stood for hundreds of years. The air was filled with the smell of charcoal fires under pots of stew.

"Along the way, we came across a group of young men playing soccer under the lights. We sat and watched and were later joined by an elderly man dressed in a long white robe and turban.

"I had noticed him watching us since the moment we sat. He appeared to be particularly interested in the flow of words between us and how Matt would ask a question and I would answer.

"He approached, speaking English, asking if he could join us and where we were from.

"'Please do,' I responded. 'My son and I are from the United States. We are here to learn about a place we've never been to and people we have yet to know. Are you Turkish?'

"'No! I am Kurdish. There are many millions of Kurdish people living here. The Turks call us an insurgent group because we demand greater autonomy along with more political and cultural rights. We want an independent Kurdistan.'

"He then looked at Matthew, saying, 'I watched you both talking. You appear to have many questions, and this intrigued me. You are young, and it is good to have questions. I am very old and have discovered many answers and many more questions along the years. I will share, if your father allows me.'

"He looked at me for approval.

"'We'd be honored! I want my son to hear many voices,' I said.

"He turned his attention to Matthew and spoke, 'You are a young man, and you have a father to teach you. Once you know who you really are, don't let anyone or anything make you be what you are not. I am a Kurd. Kurds have our own beliefs, music we listen to, foods we eat, and way we live. I am a stranger here without those things. That makes this the place I live but not my home!

"'These streets have seen the blood of armed conflicts as those in power demand we pray like them, dress like them, and live like them. We will not! We are not them!

"'I am me, and I deserve the respect of being me. Knowing who you really are means everything! It is the living truth.

"'There are forces that want to steal your identity, young man. No country on earth is immune to the diseases of ignorance, greed, and power! Knowing deep in your bones who you are and demanding the right to remain who you are is the light in this world of differences.

"'Diversity is to be cherished. We must celebrate it, learn from it, and then choose to incorporate the best teachings into our lives but never let it be forced upon you! It must be a choice, or it is criminal. Make sure you demand and offer truth! Teachings based on lies bring an end to civilization, just like teachings that are out of sync with nature.'

"He turned his eyes to me and said, 'Thank you for letting me speak! I am tired and must go now. You might consider going as well. The streets are not safe after midnight, and I want you to be safe. I want your son to grow up and continue to ask important questions!'

"I thanked this Kurd for his words of wisdom, and we wandered back to our hotel where we sat in the dimly lit lobby, talking about the brief encounter and what his words meant to us.

"Thirty minutes later, the night desk clerk served us two glasses of meet raki, sometimes called lion's milk, a national drink of twice-distilled grapes and aniseed, saying, 'I like the things you are talking about!'

"I said to Matt, 'This is why your mother and I place such importance on travel. There are treasures out there that are not in museums, and it's up to you to find them!'"

MOTORCYCLE MEMORY

Gordon had not made a sound while I was talking. There had been no questions, or even a groan.

Eventually, I stopped for gas and to stretch my legs. I walked around the parking lot under the searing Arizona sun and returned to the car.

Gordon seemed to be gone. I knew his presence was all in my head, animating memories that would not be silenced, giving them life in my false reality. I wondered if the real Gordon was still in the coma but wouldn't let myself think anything worse.

I got back on the highway and thought about the times I'd ridden my motorcycle across country. Gordon loved those stories, so I decided to keep talking despite his silence, hoping that my words might prompt a response.

"Once, while in the middle of the Mojave Desert, I got off the main road and toured the driest lands in the American Southwest, following signs for a biker bar. It was 117 degrees, and I was more than ready to get out of the saddle and into some air-conditioning.

"About twenty-five miles from the highway, I finally spotted the place up ahead on the left. It was a freestanding structure that looked as if it was left over from a John Ford-Western. Nothing but sand and cacti for miles and then this relic sits there in the dust, surrounded by a wraparound porch and about thirty motorcycles.

"I parked my white Honda Goldwing right in front of the double doors, pulled the helmet off, trudged up the steps, and entered.

"Every single head in the place turned to look at me as I crossed the worn wooden planks and put my helmet on the bar. The bartender, wearing a black patch over one eye, a red bandanna, and skull-and-crossbones tattoos on both arms, said in a questioning tone, 'I didn't hear you pull up.'

"'My bike's pretty quiet for an 1800 cc touring model,' I responded as he and the rest of the occupants stretched to look out at my ride.

"'That's not a Harley,' he exclaimed, opening up the palms of his hands as if to say, 'What the hell?' in sign language.

"It suddenly dawned on me that I had I'd stumbled into a world of its own in the middle of the desert and had broken the rules without knowing what they were.

"All eyes turned in his direction as he shouted, 'I'm not serving anything to a Japanese-kissing Honda-fucking pussy!'

"Now their eyes returned to me to see if and how I might respond.

"I was hot, I was sweaty, and I was tired. I'd been riding for eleven hours and was not in the mood for any shit. I scanned the crowd slowly, taking in the wide variety of black leather, and silver-buckled accessories, and then placed my stare directly on the bartender.

"'Listen carefully! I'll talk real slow! I know you're nearly deaf from trying to ride one of those loud ugly motherfucking toys out there, but I ride a man's bike, and this man wants a large cold motherfucking beer. *Now!*'

"Well, the entire place broke into fits of laughter, hoots, and hollers! It had all been for show, and I had played my part with an extemporaneous flare that kept the beer flowing for the next three hours without my spending a cent.

"We told biking stories and biking jokes and biking lies until I had to leave before I traded my Honda for a Harley.

"Now it was dark but not much cooler, and I needed a motel room badly. Though I'd received multiple invitations to crash on different couches, I chose to follow their directions to the Dead Horse Motel. I woke the manger from a sound sleep and signed the registry. He said it wasn't necessary, but I did it anyway as I asked for the key.

"'There ain't no key, Mr. Page,' he responded while reading my name. 'I gave up on keys years ago. Keys get lost, and I've had to break into rooms too many times. We're in the middle of frigging nowhere. The door closes. That should be enough. You'll be in cottage number six, just pull the door shut when you leave.'

"I paid him the twenty bucks in cash, just like the sign on the counter stated and then found my way in the dark to number six. There was one dim naked bulb in a lamp on the nightstand. The sheets looked fresh, but I didn't believe the rest of the place had been cleaned since the mid-1950s. I really didn't care, but I was beginning to care about getting something to eat. After using the under-attended toilet, I went back to the office to inquire about food.

"'I'd like to get something to eat before settling in for the night. Any possibilities?'

"'You're shitting me! You're going to spend the night? Most of my guests are here for about an hour!'

"'Food?' I questioned.

"'Down the road about a mile,' he answered. 'On the right-hand side! It's a truck stop. A lot of my customers come from there. The food's pretty good. They're open all night, and the service is very friendly! If you get a waitress named Sheila, tell her she still owes me forty bucks.'

"'Will do,' I said and walked away, hearing him mumble. 'All night! This keeps up, and I'll have to raise the price!'

"Sheila was my waitress, but I didn't pass on the message. She wore a standard waitress uniform that had been substantially shortened, high heels, and fishnet stockings. Her shoulder-length hair was purple and blue and orange with blond roots.

"The place smelled like last week's order of liver and onions and the jukebox was preloaded with Patsy Cline and Johnny Cash hits.

"While Sheila listened to me ask for the chicken special, I could feel her eyes scanning me for possibilities.

"'Is that every single thing you want, honey?' she asked coyly, batting her mascara-caked eyelashes with every syllable as if we'd already established some connection.

"'Oh, I almost forgot,' I added. 'I need a toasted ham and cheese for my wife, and this order's to go!'

"I didn't want to inspire any further exchange and had discovered through years of road trips that this tactic was an immediate deal breaker.

"I ate my chicken special and my wife's meal back at the motel, wishing Terry was with me to laugh at the situation."

LAUGHTER AND LOVE

Years earlier when I'd shared that motorcycling story with Gordon, he laughed loud and long, demanding I tell it again word for word. He laughed at this telling, but his laughter was not nearly as hearty, saying that laughter always made him feel as if he was healing.

He said the most critical thing that was missing in hospitals and the entire medical community was humor. This is one topic on which we both agreed.

Gordon said, "Doctors' offices and waiting rooms are similar to funeral homes and emphasized grieving more than healing. The space is dark and usually windowless, cluttered with scary-looking equipment that projects a feeling of a torture chamber.

"Even the walls are covered with posters of skeletons and fleshless muscles. Nothing that promotes a sense of humanity or beauty is present, and there is no expression of laughter to be found anywhere!

"Don't these idiots read history? Everyone knows that there was always a jester in the king's court! Laughter is essential to well-being. If you want to plant the seeds of health and hope, make somebody laugh, for God's sake!"

"That's why I wanted Mary in Sony's life," I told Gordon. "As your sister aged, she had a tendency to become sullen. Mary could break through that and get Sony laughing hysterically. This was even the case as Sony slipped into the depths of her Alzheimer's. Mary provided good and necessary medicine.

"Once, while Sony, Mary, and I were filming a short script I wrote called *Peeling Oranges*, Mary got your sister laughing so uncontrollably that we had to shut down production for the day. They couldn't even look at each other without cracking up. I found such joy in the hysteria that I kept the camera rolling. Now all these years later, I have proof of Sony's happiness."

Suddenly, after many miles of silence, Gordon struggled to speak, cleared his throat, and tried again.

"How do you continue to find joy in the midst of tragedy?" Gordon asked in a weak and raspy voice. It had been hours since his lasts words, and I wondered if thoughts of his sister's happiness had called him back.

"It's my duty," I responded, not realizing how much I sounded like my father. "I have been through a lot of shit, but even in the shittiest of times, there is humor!"

"I need an example," he murmured. "And speak a little louder. I can hardly hear you."

"Walking was difficult at best, following the stroke. I had tremendous problems moving in a straight line. Even going from the kitchen to the family room might include a collision with any number of pieces of furniture.

"I shared this with my physical therapist, who suggested that I try going to a track and jogging to see if the momentum would help. I was fearful of falling but gave it a try. It seemed to improve some things, but because of the extreme weakness on my right side, I found I could only stay on the circular track while going in a clockwise direction.

"When I told my speech therapist I was doing this, she said I should take this opportunity to verbally reach out to people I might see in order to practice my emerging language skills.

"This scared me more than the thought of falling. I never knew for sure what would come out of my mouth other than drool. She advised me to practice short concise statements and then put them into practice while jogging. She said to start with things like, 'Good morning. Nice day,' and go on from there.

"The third day that I was at the track, awkwardly jogging in my sneakers and shorts, a woman wearing a hot-pink sweatshirt passed me in the opposite direction. On her sweatshirt was printed the image of two large teddy bears. I decided that if we passed each other again, I would say, 'Nice teddy bears.' It was just three words, and I felt confident that I could spit them out correctly if I practiced for the next quarter mile.

"So I began repeating: Nice teddy bears. Nice teddy bears. Nice teddy bears. Then I practiced with volume: Nice teddy bears. Nice teddy bears. Nice teddy bears. Then I practiced with volume and a smile as I saw her coming around the bend: Nice teddy bears. Nice teddy bears. Nice teddy bears. Now she was coming right at me. She was fifty feet away and then twenty feet away. I took a huge breath and just as we were about to pass, shouted, 'Nice titties dear!'

"I thought I'd die. I had no idea where those words came from. I lost control of my running and went cross-country, offtrack as I heard her yell, 'And I like your legs!'

"Humor is everywhere, like beauty and healing, but a person must learn to hear it and see it and feel it in order to reap its benefits."

"Is this another one of your feel-good philosophies?" Gordon choked out as if he was coming out of a deep sleep.

"It's the core of everything I believe!"

"I believe nice titties can do miracles!"

"What kind of statement is that?"

"That was humor, you asshole. Open yourself up to it. Breathe it in. Let my comic discourse heal your suffering brain," Gordon said, rallying his energy with a laugh.

"That nap seems to have done you some good. When will you find the humor in your own life?"

"When pigs fly, dear brother! That's a reference from a great play, *The Lion in Winter*! It's a gift to you from me!"

"I accept it! I spoke those words when I played the part of King Henry. That play contains some of the darkest humor I've ever read.

"I've always considered humor a gift, no matter the shade. It's my go-to gift when face to face with the recipient. It's also cheap!"

"Very funny! I never know what to give anybody, no matter what the cost.

"Gift giving gets tricky! I hate looking through catalogues, and wandering up and down department store aisles with my wheelchair is a nightmare! Then there are all the questions: Should it be practical, something just for fun, something expected, or a surprise?

"I used to go crazy picking the right gift for Sony. Usually, it would be a book or antique or piece of art. I wanted every gift to communicate my feelings."

"I saw every gift you sent her, and I think you did fine!"

"I hope so. I never told her I loved her. Those words weren't in my family's vocabulary."

"When you choose the right gift, whether it's a thing, time, money, or an experience, it sends a powerful message. Your gifts did that! Sony knew how you felt!"

"Have you ever struggled to figure out what is the right gift to give?"

"A thousand times! It's tough to get it right. I've missed the mark more often than not! I remember once when the gift I chose was absolutely perfect! It happened almost by accident. I didn't even know I was looking for a gift!"

"Tell me about it," Gordon mumbled, barely audible as he began the slide back into his fog, adding, "Don't be offended if I doze. I can't quite keep my brain focused. Pretend I'm paying attention."

"I always do! By the way, that was a joke."

THE GIFT

"I was driving slowly one day on the way home from school. I was trying to put some distance between the kids waiting for me at home and the kids I'd just left at the junior high. I needed to relax, rejuvenate, and readjust.

"The day had been what we called twenty years ago crazy and what we now call normal. The classroom was a minefield that I traversed a thousand times that day, and I ached from head to toe, especially toe.

"I'd started with my lesson plans and good intentions and eye on the clock but found it near impossible to keep the juggling going. Despite being armed with degrees and practical experience and inside information on IQs and levels of disabilities and giftedness and health problems and rumors, all the answers never seemed to be there at the same time. I never knew exactly what they needed or what to give.

"Driving out of town through suburbia and into the country, I tried to look as far as I could into the distance, catching the horizon here and there between houses and trees. It felt good to see to the end of something far away after spending the day looking so close into the immediate needs of the moment, blinded by the rush of it all.

"Homeroom was a flurry of paperwork, passes to the office and to guidance counselors and therapists. I gave students their locker combinations for the twentieth time, lent money for emergency phone calls, took attendance, listened to the pledge sound like scrambled eggs, and held my breath. The bell rang, and they were off in a hairspray-scented tumble of book bags and high-tops, sweatpants, and cleavage. It ended not nearly so tidy, and I just couldn't wait to get home to my own kids.

"Matt, my middle son, had been on my mind during the day in between sit down and listen up. I'd caught a glimpse of him staring over to the old empty doghouse. There was a leftover look in his eyes when he turned to wave goodbye.

"Backing down the drive that morning, I couldn't figure out what was bothering me. I felt good. I was on time. I'd eaten and was even half awake. It wasn't until three or four miles down the road that I realized it was the picture of Matt's haunting look that was keeping my focus from being on the road. There was sadness there, a grieving, a love, an I'll-never-forget-you-*ever* kind of look. I couldn't figure out what to give him either.

"Seven fifteen was coming up fast, and I slid that picture away and started rooting for the stuff that had to be at my fingertips: abused-children stuff, alcoholic-parent stuff, sex stuff, drug stuff, police stuff, pregnancy stuff, cult stuff, violence, prejudice, overeating, underachieving, unmotivated, misbehaving, constipating stuff, and the stuff I was supposed to teach too. The day was a blur.

"I started thinking about Matt on my way home that evening because I thought I could concentrate then, at the end of the day, and understand that look a little better, but the picture kept mingling with the events of the day and other faces and other looks.

"There had been a fight in the hall before noon and tears in the restroom. Someone had their purse stolen from the gym locker and found empty in the dumpster outside. There had been a gun on the bus and police in the building before the morning bell. Vandals had expressed their anger with a flourish of spray paint, and three more windows were broken. Someone said one of the lavatories was covered with blood. I don't know whose. I don't know why. I do know that I missed my turn going home that night.

"I hadn't really been thinking about driving. It had been happening automatically while I was still piecing together noise and crowds and chunks of the curriculum to make up the memory and meaning of the day. It had been happening despite my search for the miracle that would make the next day different, special, and wonderful.

"I could have taken the next turn and turned again and been home at four thirty instead of four forty, but I didn't. I drove to the SPCA. I thought maybe I'd just look and see if there was a pair of eyes that might be a match for Matt's. I knew it was crazy. Life was already complicated. It was tough enough keeping up with kid mess, much less puppy mess. As I pulled into the parking lot, I told myself that vets are expensive, that dogs shed, that they don't come house broken, that they bark, and before I knew it, I was walking out, carrying this seven-week-old ball of fur with eyes.

"The drive back to the house was with great anticipation. He quivered on my lap, not knowing where he was going, what was happening, or who would take care of him. I stroked his head over and over, long, strong, soft, relaxing strokes and thought about Matt.

"As soon as I parked the car, I spotted him in the yard down by the fence by himself, tossing a ball high in the air and catching it. I pulled the puppy under my coat and walked toward him, yelling with my fiercest teacher voice, 'Matt, get over here. There's something I want you to take care of right now!' He dropped the ball and came running, all eyes.

When he was right in front of me, all scared and unsure and looking guilty and sorry and everything, he asked, 'Take care of what?'

"'This,' I said, letting the little nose push the coat open and jump right into Matt's hands. He cried, hugged me, thanked me, and told me he couldn't believe it.

"The next day, driving to school, I kept thinking about Matt and his face when he first saw the puppy, and I never quite got thinking about the stuff that usually starts my day. Even during first period, I started to tell the story about the puppy 'cause it was just on my mind.

"There I was, standing in the midst of unbroken silence, talking about a puppy hidden under a coat and a lonesome kid. No tattooed arm shoved, no painted mouth yelled, no notes were passed, no jokes were made, no blood was shed, but there were tears. And they wanted to hear it again and again, and I told it over and over, slow and strong, stroking them with my words, and they got really calm, really quiet.

"Period after period, I repeated that story, even wearing the coat for affect. Each new group clambered in before the bell, begging for the puppy story. I must have given away a hundred puppies that day. It was a miracle, different, and special. It felt wonderful!"

Gordon didn't say a word but that was okay. He was tired.

CALIFORNIA

California was the next border for me to cross, and the closer I got, the further away it felt. I kept thinking about what I could possibly give Gordon that would make a difference.

The traffic was getting heavy, and the need to concentrate on the road demanded more attention than I was able to muster. I preferred the open space of the desert where my mind could wander a little without jeopardizing any lives. I tried to pull back from the seductive powers of my own memories, but even with increased coffee stops and tuning into multiple different radio stations at full volume, I'd slip away, finding myself in dreams of yesterdays.

I found myself with Gordon in Laguna Beach, scouting out new art galleries and chic restaurants. Then we were strolling the windblown coastal sidewalk, watching the shirtless muscled life guards and tanned bikini beauties showing off their volleyball skills along with everything else.

Later, I was driving Gordon's van through the steep hills and winding roads that lead to neighborhoods with multimillion-dollar houses, featuring spectacular views of the shoreline, white surf, and a glimpse of Catalina Island in the distance.

Then there were memories of trips to LA, the Tar Pits, the Getty Museum, and Grumman's Chinese Theater. There were many evenings spent in the wine bar at the Irvine Spectrum Center, followed by a movie and getting a pizza to take home.

There were multiple drives along the Pacific Coast Highway, stops at Fashion Island, and visits to all the famous beaches, like Malibu, Santa Monica, and Venice.

We even toured the Queen Mary, which is permanently docked in Long Beach. This is the ship that carried my father home from World War II along with thousands of soldiers who were fortunate enough to survive that particular hell.

Standing on the deck of that ship, I tried to imagine what it must have been like for my father to have left this country as a boy and come back a man who had been shoulder deep in some of the most tragic events in history. I felt ashamed that I didn't understand him better when I was young.

Gordon and I also drove to Palm Springs, toured the Salt Flats, and spent hours visiting San Juan Capistrano. We were intrigued by the many antique shops, restaurants, and the famous Spanish mission along with its surrounding gardens.

We attended the Sawdust Art Festival numerous times, always coming home with a few treasures that now hung in Gordon's house beside his own artwork.

I even got Gordon on a boat to Catalina Island where I rented a golf cart, strapped him in, and spent the day exploring every cove and interesting rock formation. We were like two kids in a go-kart, breaking every rule, faces full of sun and wind and laughter.

I recalled our train ride to San Diego, the zoo, Balboa Park, and the remarkable Hotel del Coronado where the movie *Some Like It Hot* was filmed.

Then there was the very first time visiting Gordon, following the stroke. I was not in the best shape, and he was recovering from a recent bladder infection. We were both tired and decided to forgo local adventures for multiple trips to the movies.

Even getting Gordon into the van to the theater and home again was a challenge. My right hand was still trying to cling to my chest, and my fingers couldn't feel the straps and buckles needed to tie his wheelchair down to the floor of the van. The sudden thunderstorm and multiple lightning strikes didn't make the situation any easier.

We always left the house early so we could get our tickets quickly and find a place in the disabled section without difficulties. This section had a small area without a seat where Gordon could park his electric chair nearest the aisle next to where I could sit.

Of course, this meant we'd have to suffer through previews and a long wait, but the popcorn helped fill the gap. Eventually, the theater would fill, the lights would dim, and the movie would begin. A thirty-something man sat to my left, just as the film began.

Ten minutes before the film's end, just as the lead character was about to win the girl's heart, defeat her evil stepfather, and save the day, the bright and dazzling images disappeared from the screen as the entire theater fell into blackness.

"My god," shrieked the guy next to me, "that was like bad sex. All that sweat, and for what? Freaking nothing!"

Just as the laugher settled down, the theater manager, with flashlight in hand, spoke from in front of the screen. "There's been a power failure along with some other technical difficulties! We apologize for the inconvenience, but you will have to come back at a later date to view the film in its entirety. Please pick up your tickets in the lobby as soon as we get the emergency lights to function. We appreciate you remaining in your seats for safety reasons for a few extra minutes."

Those few extra minutes turned into a half an hour, sitting in absolute blackness as the guy next to us went on and on and on about how this was the last straw and that he didn't think he could take any more. He shared how he had run out of gas on the way to pick up his date. Then while rushing to get her, he got a speeding ticket, so he canceled the date and came to the movies alone where he ran into his ex-wife and her boyfriend in the lobby. He was just saying, "Jesus Christ! Why does everything happen to me?" as the lights came back on, and he saw us, twisted, drooling—us, the picture of what a bad day really looks like!

His jaw dropped! He stared! He jumped up and ran to the opposite aisle, bolting up to the lobby doors, falling twice along the way.

Gordon and I almost pissed ourselves laughing!

I changed the radio station every time I finished a short memory but then another one would pop into my head. Each thought was like a stone being skipped across the surface of a pond, splashing down for a second and then splashing down in another place again and again and again with the distance between splashdowns lessening with each episode.

In Riverside, I stopped for more gas and a chance to break the chain of recollections that was jamming my head. I took a short walk and then called the hospital and was told that Gordon was just beginning to come around.

The need to be there when Gordon woke gave me a renewed focus, and I was able to drive to Saddleback Hospital without distractions.

We were both coming back to reality at the same time, and I would be there to meet him!

BEDSIDE

I was at his bedside when he opened his eyes. He saw me, smiled, and spoke in a soft, weak whisper, "Thanks for the puppy," before drifting back into dreams.

I'll never know how he knew about the puppy. I'd never told him that story.

The doctor said that Gordon would not be fully ready to maintain consciousness until the next day. With real concern, he also said I looked like hell and recommended a shower and sleep. I did feel a little beat up, so I headed to Gordon's house and collapsed.

In my exhaustion, I found myself reliving a conversation I once had with Gordon. He was showing me all the things he had purchased and stored in his garage in case of an earthquake. There was a generator, thermal blankets, a container holding one hundred gallons of filtered water, freeze-dried meats, soups, vegetables, and fruits along with a collection of flashlights, batteries, flares, and medications.

"I'm afraid of earthquakes," Gordon said. "I want to be prepared, but in reality, all this stuff I've got stored here are things I can't even get to. It's all for nothing, if somebody isn't here to help me."

"I'll get here on the first plane."

"I'll be dead by the time you reach me. Quakes break gas lines. There're always fires! I'll burn to death in that fucking bed, smelling my flesh broil in my own juices."

"That's disgusting, but thanks for sharing such a unique vision. Now I'm sure to sleep well tonight."

"Sorry, but I think about it all the time."

"Then why do you live in Southern California? There are fault lines everywhere. Seismologists have been saying for over a hundred years, 'The *big one is coming*!'"

"Thanks for the reminder. Now neither one of us will sleep!"

"So why here? It's a big country."

"This climate is fantastic for quads! People like me can't tolerate extremes. Quads come from all over the world to live here. Although the roads are crowded, they're well maintained, and the sidewalks are great! I have an element of freedom here. I'm close to one of the best Veteran's Hospitals in the nation, and they happen to specialize in treating my condition."

"Makes sense!"

"Besides, I'll probably kick the bucket before the *big one*!"

"Well, there's a comforting thought!"

"What scares you?"

"You mean other than you kicking the bucket or becoming barbecued?"

"Yes! What keeps you up at night besides having to pee?"

"I worry about my wife and kids and grandkids. I want them to have long, healthy, happy, and productive lives. I pray for them every night."

"You pray?"

"All the time! Perhaps it's not in the traditional way, but it's in a way that works for me."

"Does it work for God?"

"I haven't had any complaints, and the family is doing well. That's what counts!"

"They mean everything to you, don't they?"

"More than my own life! I couldn't bear to lose any one of them! Terry and I lost our first child before he was even born. In the last stages of pregnancy, Terry got the flu, and the high fever resulted in the baby's death."

"Don't you mean the death of the fetus?"

"No! He was a baby to us! We named him Jason Charles. Charles was my father's name. Jason was and always will be our first son. We loved him! At night, I'd lay my head on Terry's swollen belly and tell him so. I sang to him. I dreamed of him, I loved him, and when he died, I thought I'd die. It was the greatest pain I ever felt, the darkest moment of my existence, the worst day of my life."

"Worse than the stroke?"

"No comparison! I cannot lose another child!"

"You never told me about Jason before."

"Some stories are hard to tell. Terry and I talk of him. That love still lives!"

"I have never known that kind of love. I only have me, broken, battered, and bruised. Just me!"

"How often do I have to say it? You've got me."

"That's like saying I've got a pimple on my ass."

"Very funny."

"All joking aside, are Jason's ashes in the garden?"

"He was so tiny! There were no ashes for us to bury. I wrote a poem, and when my mother died, I slipped it into her coffin before they closed the lid. They're together."

"Sounds like a useless effort in sentimentality."

"It was a symbolic gesture."

"Prayers! Symbolism! What about science and concrete facts?"

"I don't think prayers and science contradict each other. Science has a great deal to do with searching the unknown to solve long-standing mysteries. Prayers seem very similar."

"I have my doubts."

"You're allowed! Doubts can be the seed of an investigation, or even a prayer."

"Don't get me wrong. If I don't end up in your garden, I'll come back and haunt you! I might anyway, just to scare the shit out of you!"

"If you do, will you be walking?"

"That's my prayer."

GORDON'S DRAWINGS

When I woke the next morning, I couldn't quite get my bearings. I rolled over, scanned my surroundings, recognized the room I had known for decades, and still felt lost. I got up, showered, dressed, walked into Gordon's room and around the entire house. I was thinking about all the things he'd directed me to take care of in the event of his death. It seemed more real than ever before, and I didn't like the feeling.

I looked at his vast collection of books and the artwork he'd assembled over the years. Then I stared in depth at each of his drawings and thought about the thousands of hours of disciplined concentration that had gone into the studying of and execution of each piece. It all seemed unimaginable, yet there they were, all those famous people looking out from Gordon's walls without a single blink, without a single word, without knowing that a stranger with every reason to never pick up a pencil had done so to bring their image into his world!

How I wished that each of them could have sat with Gordon while he drew their portrait. I could just imagine the conversations and laughter. I stood in front of each piece and called their name out loud, like I was calling the troops to attention back in the Army: "Whoopi Goldberg! Anthony Hopkins! Grace Slick! Al Pacino! Truman Capote! Gillian Anderson! Willie Nelson! Clint Eastwood! Diana Ross! Peter Sellers! Igor Stravinsky! Fidel Castro! John Ford! David Bowie! Robert Mitchum! Jack Nicholson! Bruce Willis! Sissy

Spacek! Isabelle Adjani! Mick Jagger! Eric Clapton! Denis Hopper! Rickie Lee Jones! Dizzy Gillespie! Lucille Ball! Bob Marley!" Their names echoed through the house, and then silence returned with a vengeance.

Hospital visiting hours started at ten, so I ran from the silence as if I was being chased. I stopped at the local Starbucks where I would sometimes meet Gordon's friend Steve. He was not there on that particular morning, and I missed his friendly face and intelligent insights.

Steve visited Gordon often and was a true friend. They would sit out on the patio, drinking beer and talking about books and films and politics. I was always grateful that Gordon had a comrade like this who could equal his intellect and present challenging opinions.

Steve represented a rare mix of interests and expertise. He studied religion, theater, and film; and his communication skills were excellent, especially his ability to listen. I could have used a good listener that morning at Starbucks. I had much to say and needed some feedback.

I sat alone with my coffee, watching some of the regulars who I'd become familiar with over the years.

There was always this man who would order a coffee grande and sit outside by himself for an hour, scratching off the little silver squares on the dozens of lottery tickets he'd purchased. He was there every day that I went to that Starbucks. Even if I didn't stop but only drove by, he'd be there in the same spot doing the same thing. I don't know if he ever won anything. He never changed his routine, or expression. He'd just methodically scratch each card, slowly, carefully, examining every detail as if it were a piece of art. I wondered if it was all he ever did, and I wondered if his scraping away was like Gordon's filling in the grids for his drawings, hoping for a winner.

Hospital Number 1

They were just raising the back of Gordon's bed when I entered his room. He was very thin and white as the pillow cradling his head. His eyes were bloodshot and voice raspy.

"I thought I remembered seeing you but wasn't sure if it was a dream or not."

"It's me. I drove out to California!"

"I wish I'd been with you."

"You were!"

"David, my head has been full of memories. You were in those dreams and Terry. So was Sony. I remember seeing my nurse! It all seemed so real!

"Is my nurse here?"

"There are a lot of nurses here."

"I mean my special nurse from years ago! Is she here?" he questioned and began to choke for a moment while straining to look out the open door.

"Be still, Gordon. You've been through a lot and need to rest."

"I thought I heard her laughing.

"Is Terry here?"

"Not this time. She sends her love and said she'll come out when you're ready for an adventure."

"Good! That will give me something to look forward to!"

"So what's going on? When you called me last week, you sounded good."

"Same old shit! The doctor says I'm wearing out!"

"Is that the exact medical term?"

"It's my interpretation! The medical terms mask the fact that things are getting worse. My bladder is failing along with other major organs. I'm also having severe spasms."

"Like the ones you had years ago?"

"Worse! They can't even find the cause. I had one while I was drawing and nearly destroyed a piece I've put hundreds of hours into. I won't be able to finish it!"

"How close to being done is it?"

"Just like me, it's as close as it's ever going to be."

Gordon looked slowly around the room, taking in all the equipment, analyzing the technical adequacy, and determining if his needs could be met.

"Can I get you anything? Do you need anything? Do you want anything?"

"Yes! I want you to get me the hell out of here! This particular hospital is great, but I need some specialized care that they can't deliver. Can you get me transferred?"

"I can try! Do you have a preference? Where can you get the best care?"

"The Veteran's Hospital! I know it means that you will have to drive into the LA traffic for visits, but they have the kind of mattress a quad needs in order to prevent bedsores and the experts who can give this old body proper care. Can you help me?"

"If I liked you at all, I might consider it, but—"

Gordon smiled and asked, "How long can you stay in California?"

"As long as it takes! I'll start making phone calls right away.

"Your job is to heal. I'll take care of the rest."

I hugged his frail bony body and left on a mission, far different from driving across the country and much more complicated. I had no map, or background for this excursion.

Help

I didn't know where to begin, so I went to the social services department for information, fearful of the bureaucratic walls I might have to climb and manufacturing roadblocks and detours that might not be there. As it turned out, all my fears were justified, but I was not alone in facing them.

The woman in charge was fantastic! She gave me her full and undivided attention. She had spunk and a great face framed by a massive amount of unruly hair that she kept pushing this way and that way as she talked.

Instead of just giving me a list of numbers to call, she offered to call, saying, "I know how to cut through the mountains of paperwork and crap that can delay this forever. Sit here with me as I make some inquiries! You said Gordon's your brother?"

"We see it that way."

She looked up from the pile of files she'd already assembled, saying, "Explain," as she put the phone back on the receiver.

"He's my friend! We've been friends for forty years."

"Are you his legal power of attorney?"

"I am, and I have the paperwork right here," I responded while handing her the documents.

"I'll have these copied while you start filling out the transfer forms. Get comfortable. You're going to be here for a while. Because you are not a blood relative, the powers that be will want to know just about everything. Do you have a criminal record?" she suddenly asked without any tonal changes in her voice as if she was asking for my phone number.

"Clean as a whistle," I answered.

"Good. That will make this a lot easier!"

"Out of curiosity, why would you ask that?"

"Oh, you would be surprised how many veterans, especially ones like your friend, are taken advantage of by healthcare aides, neighbors, and others who want their house, their vehicle, their insurance, their belongings, and their money. It's a big racket and that is why everything needs to be done by the book. It can't be rushed, or it will draw legal attention."

"I had no idea!"

"Does Gordon have a legal and recent will, and are you the beneficiary?"

"Yes, and yes."

"Having the will is great, but being one who might benefit by his passing will make this more difficult. Employed?"

"I'm a retired school administrator. Now I am a writer and artist."

"Where do you live?"

"Pennsylvania!"

She looked up from the notes she'd been taking, leaned back in her office chair, rocking back and forth slowly as she studied me carefully.

"So you are supposedly a friend from out of state, not a blood relative but Gordon's beneficiary?"

"And I'm driving his car and staying in his house! Do I need a lawyer?"

"Mr. Page, is your name on any of Gordon's bank accounts?"

"Sure! I've been helping Gordon out for years. He's a quad! Are you suggesting—"

"I'm not suggesting anything! I'm showing you just how hard this is going to be. Yes, call your lawyer now right here from my office while I'm sitting here," she said as she handed me the phone. I stood to accept the phone and the challenge.

I immediately recognized this as a test of legitimacy and knew I'd never be able to maneuver the bureaucracy without help from the inside. I called the lawyer, put the phone on speaker mode, and stated where I was, what I was attempting to do, reviewed my relationship with Gordon, and communicated his current situation. The lawyer charged three hundred dollars an hour, including phone calls, so I was brief. As soon as I hung up the phone, the inquisitor across the desk, stood, took off her glasses, came to where I was standing, and hugged me, saying, "You passed!" From that point on, we were a team, and I never could have done what had to be done without her.

It took almost two hours to fill out half the forms and sign the required documents. A person with a fully functioning right hand could have done it in a quarter of that time, but since the stroke, holding a pen and writing anything legible is nearly impossible and very painful. I shared this with my office teammate and she asked me, "How in the world can you be an artist and writer?"

"Working with a paintbrush is easier for me because I concentrate on the bend of the bristles at the end of the brush to determine the pressure to be applied. I break pens and pencils by the dozens. As for the writing, a keyboard is another challenge. I have zero feelings on my right side and must feel through my eyes to find the correct keys to strike. Of course, none of this is anything compared to what my friend has wrestled with."

She looked up, shook her head, and dove back into files, forms, and frustrations, saying, "In the middle of all this shit, you made my day!"

While I struggled with the paperwork, she made multiple phone calls and arrangements. She was brilliant at concisely communicating the facts and the need for expediency. When things were not moving in the right direction, she'd ask for that person's manager. If she couldn't get satisfaction from the manager, she'd demand to talk with the supervisor. At one point, she had the director of the hospital on the line!

Eventually, she hung up and shared the plan.

"I'll give you the bad news first."

"That's the way I like it!"

"There is not one single bed available in the spinal care unit at the Veteran's Hospital, and there's a substantial waiting list."

"Is there more bad news, or can we move on to the good stuff?"

"Oh, there's more! The VA will only accept just so many transfers from any one particular hospital. Our hospital has temporarily exceeded our limit!"

"Where does that leave us, or are we screwed?"

"The only way you really get screwed in this world is not having enough lawyers, or giving up before you learn how to play the game!"

"Do I get the lawyer back on the phone?"

"Hell no! You go get something to eat and meet me here in about an hour."

"Can I take you out for lunch?"

"Thanks, but, no! I've got to work fast. When somebody tells me that there's no possible way, I get completely turned on, so get your blue eyes out of here before I get distracted."

"But—"

"Go!" she shouted, pointing at the door. "And don't eat in the cafeteria. I don't want to be searching for a second hospital bed."

I took the elevator down to street level, feeling guilty as if I'd tossed my heavy load to a stranger and left. I spotted a little eatery within walking distance and headed in that direction, feeling the lightness of having put the weight on someone else's shoulder.

THE STROKE

As I walked, I reflected on my own hospital stay, following the stroke. I was incredibly confused and disoriented. I could remember coming home from a production of *Romeo and Juliet*. It was late, and I was tired.

I got a glass of water and turned on the television to watch the news. I silenced the volume in order to keep from disturbing my sleeping family. The Oklahoma bombing had just taken place, and I was about to sit when the glass fell from my hand and rolled across the floor, leaving a trail of water. In that same instant, I fell backward, diagonally across the couch, unable to catch myself.

My first thought was *How clumsy! I must be more tired than I thought,* but none of this was from clumsiness or being tired. I tried to move and couldn't. I tried to call out, but no sound came.

I thought, *Oh my god, I'm having a stroke!* And I was. I could not move. I watched the television images of horror and destruction in absolute silence, except for the sound of the tendons in my right hand as they knotted, cramped, and pulled my hand into an unrecognizable twisted claw that clung to my chest.

Then the same power began to rearrange the right side of my face, closing one eye and pulling my lips and chin into monstrous contortions.

I began to drool. It filled up my throat and poured out of my gaping mouth, rolled down my arm, and dripped to the floor where it joined the stream of spilled water. I began to choke! The drool was filling my airway, and panic set in. I was slowly drowning in my own spit.

I concentrated on trying to redirect breathing from my mouth to my nose in an attempt to get enough oxygen to remain conscious. Forcing one intake of air to follow another was hampered by the increasing sense of urgency and rapid heart rate.

I focused on calming down and taking as much control of this out-of-control situation as possible. Eventually, a reasonable rhythm was established, and I lay there, sprawled and drooling and scared that this could be how my wife and children might find my body in the morning.

In the corner of the living room was an antique rocking chair that began to draw my attention. It had been given to us by my wife's grandmother and was where we had cradled and rocked our babies. Behind the rocker, a soothing impossibly blue light began to appear, like a rising fog.

Somewhere in that mist, I found comfort and felt as if I was being drawn into it, becoming part of the great depth of it. In that deep well of blue/gray hypnotizing fog, I heard my mother's voice and invitation to join her.

It seemed easier than the challenge I was fighting. It felt like a possible answer. I knew that Jason was in there somewhere, and I wanted to go but then I heard a cough from upstairs, probably one of his brothers in their sleep, and suddenly, I wanted to hold them more that I wanted to leave.

The blue light began to fade, like the ending of an old motion picture in which the image shrunk into an infinitely small spot of light and then was gone.

At the same time, I began to feel a tingling sensation and a sense that I could attempt to move. With great effort and emerging pain, I rolled over and landed face-first on the floor. After a brief recovery, I squirmed to the bottom of the steps, forcing my head up to see my Everest!

Using my left elbow, knee, and foot along with my chin to guide the way and grab each step, I began to climb. It wasn't easy! I slipped in my own drool, sweat, and the blood dripping from my raw and bleeding chin.

It was two steps up and fallback, recover, and try again and again until I reached the top. Hours passed.

Periodically, I'd try calling out, but it was like a childhood nightmare in which the mouth opened, but no scream came.

Getting the length of my body onto the second-floor landing was frightening. I knew a slip would result in a fall I wouldn't recover from. Out of breath, contemplating every option, I thought about my wife asleep at the end of the hall. Just the thought of her gave me the strength to make the first move.

I pictured her on that blanket in Peter Pan Park in Kansas and saw her again, holding my hand as we crossed the Pont Neuf bridge that particular anniversary. I remembered thinking, *I am with the most beautiful woman in Paris!*

I pressed my left shoulder against the wall and slid my face across the molding and then up as I forced my screaming back upright to a locked position so I might balance on my knees. I took a big breath and let myself fall forward.

Then it was a slow and clumsy crawl down the hall past my sleeping children's bedrooms and to an impossible cliff that was the side of our bed where Terry was about to be wakened from a dream and into a nightmare.

I tried calling out, and to my surprise, I was able to make sounds, but they were not discernible.

Steadying myself with my left arm, I clenched the bedspread with my teeth. I pulled myself up, one bite at a time, stood, and fell on top of her, screaming, "I'mj hav ah stork!" I could not force myself to make sense, but clarity had come back into my head and more control over my body.

"Hospital," I spat out in a spray of saliva.

"Ambulance?" she questioned, wide-eyed and scared.

"No time! Drive!"

She got me down the stairs and into the car as I recovered more and more ability to maneuver and awkwardly speak. In minutes, we were at the emergency ward where I was able to walk in with Terry's assistance. She explained the circumstances as I wobbled on her arm.

Then I was in a wheelchair and rushed onto a gurney, followed by confusion and chaos and unconsciousness as the second stroke took the driver's seat, leaving me an unwilling passenger on the road to who knows where.

I woke the next morning filled with adrenaline-fed anxiousness. My world was a scramble of puzzle pieces that could not be forced together. Nothing made sense!

The elderly man in the bed next to me was crying out in his sleep. The only words of his I understood were "No! Oh, no. No!" That seemed to express everything that needed to be said for both of us!

I was hooked up to all kinds of machines, which rang and beeped and buzzed and flashed and dripped fluids into both arms.

I knew I was alive, but I didn't know who I was, or how old I was, what my name was, or if I was going to be alive for the next ten minutes.

Doctors came in along with a pretty woman and stood by my bed. I recognized no one, closed my eyes, and listened.

"He's had severe strokes. There's been major brain damage. The chances of recovery are slim at best."

The woman was called out of the room to sign some papers while the doctors kept talking.

"He'll never walk again or talk again or be anything more than a vegetable!"

"She might as well pray that he die," the other doctor added, "then she can get on with her life."

This was me they were talking about! That must have been my wife! They're wrong! My thoughts screamed, *I died last night! I came back. I wasn't ready then, and I'm not ready now! I have things to do!*

"Let's give him a few days to see if he stabilizes," the doctor said to his partner. "If he's still alive at that point, we'll send him home to die."

There was that word again—die. The doctors stopped speaking when my wife returned.

They only told her the part about waiting to be stabilized and that I would be coming home soon. The dying part was never mentioned.

She stood there for a long time in silence, kissed my cheek, and then left me to my imitation of sleep.

Later, someone came to give me an in-bed sponge bath. Lots of the touching hurt but only on my left side. My entire right side still slept, numb, paralyzed, and unable! I was also shaved.

After that process, the nurse held up a mirror for my approval. The twisted face shocked me!

I had wondered what I looked like. I was glad I was not as old as the man in the next bed but disappointed that I was not younger. I tried to guess my age but fell asleep.

GORDON'S ACCIDENT

In my sleep, I dreamed of Gordon and the story he only told me once of waking up in the hospital following his accident. He told me that unconsciousness had started at the moment of impact and stayed for three days. When he woke, he knew the situation was bad but did not know how bad until the specialists met and sent a member of the team to review the details of brain scans, MRIs, x-rays, and blood work with my friend.

"The good news is," the doctor said with a smile, "your neurological results are good. No brain damage at all."

"Just everything else!" Gordon responded and then asked, "Are my friends here in the same hospital? Can I see them? Are they okay?"

"Someone else will be stopping by to update you on that situation. He'll see you before you are moved to the spinal-trauma center."

Then the doctor looked at his cell phone as if he'd received an emergency call, turned his back to me, saying he'd check in later and exited. That's the moment I knew my friends were not okay. This was the largest and closest Veteran's Hospital in the area. They were all in the military. I didn't need to have some fake master of compassion or hospital chaplain explain the situation.

I knew they were injured, and I knew one of us had been driving. I remembered the black night, the rain, the construction site, squeal of brakes, and sound of crunching metal and bones! They were all young! We were all young!

The roads were wet. The lights were glaring! We'd been drinking! It was dark. The music was loud. We were on shore leave, doing what young stupid guys do. Don't they? Didn't we? Didn't I? Oh, Jesus! I don't remember anything else. Don't ask me any questions. Don't make me remember!

It was never spoken of again!

BLACK ANGEL

The second night of my hospitalization, I lay awake, trying with all my might to find the center of my being and repair the broken and damaged parts that the stroke had caused. I concentrated on the tiniest pieces of unconnected memories and images, searching for meaning.

The dim light was broken by the door to the room being swung wide open. An older black woman came into my room, quietly carrying a mop and bucket along with other cleaning materials and tools.

As the door swung shut, she went about her business, dusting and scrubbing and mopping as I watched. When she was finished, she set everything down and read my name out loud from my medical chart. It was the first time I'd heard my name, but I recognized it and was grateful to know it and feel it surround me like a warm blanket.

"David C. Page," she said out loud twice. "That name is so familiar. Do I know you?" she questioned while walking up to my pillow. She stood there, gently stroking my face and forehead as she studied my image. I had been poked and prodded and stabbed and punctured since being admitted and now this gentle and comforting touch. I began to cry as I watched her watch me.

"I do know you, Mr. David C. Page," she exclaimed. "You made me cry once while sitting in the first row of a performance of *Man of La Mancha*. Dulcinea was begging you to continue to see the world as it might be, rather than how it is. She implored you to remember the dream, and you sang. You remember? I know you remember. You must remember! I'll sing it with you."

I had no idea what she was talking about or referring to but continued to weep as she sang soft and gentle in a whisper, "To dream the impossible dream / To fight the unbeatable foe / To bear with unbearable sorrow / To run where the brave dare not go."

"Let me hear your voice again. Please, sing for me!" she urged.

As she began the last verse, I started to remember bits and pieces and struggled to sing. "And the world will be better for this / That one man scorned and covered with scars / Still strove with his last ounce of courage / To reach the unreachable star."

By the time we got to the last line, all the words were there as we sang and cried together.

She kissed me in the middle of my forehead, the way my mother used to do, saying, "I love you, David C. Page," and left.

I didn't sleep for the rest of the night. I just embraced all the connections that were flooding through my brain. Calendars with dates and files of information along with data and records and names and places filled me to the brim. I remembered my wife and sons. I remembered my parents. I remembered Gordon. I remembered Jason, and I cried!

The next morning, I struggled to ask if I could speak to the woman who cleaned my room during the night and was told, "You must be mistaken, sir! According to our records, your room isn't scheduled to be cleaned until this afternoon."

FAST FOOD

After leaving Gordon's social worker, I crossed over three parking lots, two boulevards, one highway, and three small streets, to find the place to eat I'd spotted when I left the hospital.

I wasn't feeling hungry but knew the walk would do me good.

The place was decorated in a 1950s retro look. It was all black-and-white tiles with red accents.

The staff wore black slacks, white short-sleeve tops, red bowties, and white paper hats that made them each look like they should be selling ice cream from the back of a truck. There were too many florescent lights, too many people, and too many options on the menu. A hamburger could come topped with bacon, avocados, tomatoes, onions, pickles, mushrooms, hot peppers, and something I didn't know how to pronounce. Then, of course, there were dressings that included ranch, ketchup, mustard, taco sauce, horseradish, mayonnaise, along with fifteen different types of cheese.

"Can I take your order, sir?" came the cheeriest inquiry I had ever heard. It was like holiday music. It had just the right sweetness, light and timber, delivered with perfect diction. It encouraged a customer to do mission work in a war zone to join her church, as well as her political party, and even give up sex!

I looked up to a whiter-than-white cavity-free gleaming smile that shamed the lighting system. Every tooth was braces straight, forced into perfection, and lined up at attention, like no troop of soldiers I'd ever seen.

"Never mind. I've changed my mind."

I slid off the red vinyl bar stool with the chrome base and thought I'd walk for an hour.

Unfortunately, nothing else looked any more real. The sky seemed too blue, the sun too yellow, the cars too clean.

I missed the authenticity of Mom's barbecue, dented pickup trucks, and my friend.

I hurried back to the hospital!

BROTHERS

"Good. You're back in my office just in time. Now we can get the ball rolling. Have a seat, and I'll give you the details. By the way, I went to visit your buddy. He's quite a guy, and he thinks the world of you."

"What did he have to say?"

"He confided in me! He said you've been trying to kill him for years and plan on stealing everything he has. Then he laughed like crazy."

"Yup, that's Gordon!"

"He also told me you're a chronic story teller and that I should hear a few before the transfer."

"Then I guess I'll start with some of the many embarrassing episodes of Gordon's life. That will fill up a couple of days," I responded as the smile faded from her face.

"I also talked with his doctors!" she said slowly with great compassion.

"You know that Gordon doesn't have much time left."

"Here, you mean! He doesn't have much time left here in this hospital."

"David, he doesn't have much time left anywhere!"

I knew that. I'd known that for a long time, but hearing somebody else say it was new to me. Gordon and I had always danced around the topic with jokes and wisecracks without saying, "Not much time left." I thought I was sitting, but I fell down to my knees as she stood and reached for me.

"He's always rallied before," I insisted.

She helped me into the chair and handed me a tissue.

"And maybe he will rally again, but this time, he has major organ failure, and infections are knocking on his door."

"We won't answer."

"They have a key."

"Does this mean no transfer?"

"This means we have to act fast. I have a friend at another hospital. That particular hospital has not had a transfer to the VA in three weeks. I've arranged for an ambulance to pick up Gordon and transfer him to that hospital today! The moment he has a bed in that facility, my friend will get him on the waiting list to be transferred to the VA. It's the best we can do."

"Did you share this with Gordon?"

"I did. He says if you agree, it's a go.

"Gordon's waiting for you. Give him the good news."

"Thank you for doing this for Gordon."

"I didn't do this for Gordon. I did this for brothers!"

I took the elevator up to the third floor and stood outside his room for a moment to build a believable attitude for my entrance. After a few deep breaths, I burst in.

"Guess what, buddy? We're going on a road trip!"

HOSPITAL NUMBER 2

I followed the ambulance to the new hospital and spent the first hour filling out additional paperwork and answering questions. The place was further from Gordon's home, and I had to face more highway traffic, but he was upbeat and positive because the plan was in the works. The next step would get him in the Veteran's Hospital.

The ambulance ride had exhausted Gordon. He could barely keep his eyes open as he thanked me over and over again for making it all happen.

"Listen, my friend. It wasn't just me. Lots of good people helped make this happen. Without their help, I would have turned you over to the Soylent Green Corporation."

Right away, Gordon picked up on my making a connection to one of his favorite old movies in which people were killed and made into food to feed the deeply overpopulated and starving residents of New York City.

"I think I would have made some damned good mush," Gordon responded with a chuckle.

"Unfortunately, there's just not enough meat on your bones. Put on another thirty pounds, and they might be interested."

By the time I finished that sentence, he was sound asleep. I settled into a chair and just watched him the way I've watched him for decades, amazed that he was still here, still fighting for that next moment.

Seeing him slowly drift into a deep sleep reminded me of the last time I brought Sony to California. I couldn't get tickets to the closest airport, so we had to fly into LAX.

Sony was also slipping away at that point because of the rapid depletion of her abilities brought on by Alzheimer's. She was living in a full-care facility since I was no longer able to provide the twenty-four-seven care she required.

I thought I could handle her and her brother at the same time. I was wrong!

Sony had gone downhill rapidly, and because I was no longer there every minute, I was unaware of the drastic changes that were happening daily!

I had already promised them a trip to San Diego and though lots of things were forgotten, the promise was not one of them.

She was unable to go to the restroom by herself and would often forget to tell me of her need to go. This made the flight west incredibly difficult along with eating, dressing, seat belts, appropriate language, and responses to everybody, including those serving food on the airline.

"And what can I get for you, miss?" the flight attendant asked, leaning beyond me to address Sony.

"I'd like lots and lots of chocolate ice cream and a big Coke with crushed ice. You can just keep that coming all the way to... Where are we going?" she asked me innocently. The flight attendant looked at me, smiled sweetly, and told Sony, "I love chocolate too," before hurrying away. She kept bringing Sony very small dishes of ice cream all the way to Los Angeles. She even watched over her when I needed the restroom. When I tried to thank her, she said, "No thanks necessary! My mother has dementia too. How long has your mom been ill?"

I was no stranger to people thinking Sony was my mother and just answered, "Five years," not correcting her assumption. I had become used to the fact that the disease had not only stolen Sony's mind but her looks as well. Sony appeared twenty years older than her age.

Once we landed, there was the baggage-claim hell to deal with and the car rental place and three more restroom experiences before the hour-and-a-half drive to Lake Forest. It was ten thirty in the evening when we got to Gordon's, and as soon as she saw the house, she shouted, "This is where my brother lives!" For the next hour, as we greeted Gordon and talked about the trip, she seemed perfectly fine, and I felt perfectly crazy.

When Gordon's night aide left, I got Sony ready for bed. She slept in the spare bedroom where I usually slept, and I crashed on the living room couch.

Around three in the morning, I was awakened buy noises in the kitchen and immediately ran to see what was going on. It was Sony, holding a coffee mug upside down under the running faucet and not understanding why she couldn't get a drink of water.

I finally got her settled around five, but we were up again at eight to take the train to San Diego.

It was an entire day of miracles and nightmares. I was juggling as fast as I could, trying to keep it all going despite a failing wheelchair battery, food, and bathroom mishaps. Then the return train had mechanical problems and was two-hours late for departure. This caused us to miss the night aide completely, so I had to get Gordon and Sony both ready for and into bed.

The first miracle of the day was that Sony and Gordon thought that everything was perfectly wonderful. The second miracle was that everyone survived!

I slept the rest of the week on the floor outside Sony's room to make sure she didn't wake and wander out of the house, or decide to cook something.

Watching them say goodbye was more difficult than the trip to San Diego. They hugged and wouldn't let go of each other until I repeated several times that we had a rental car to return and a plane to catch. Sony cried, saying, "I'll be back real soon!"

In the car on the way to the airport, Sony sat quietly, lost in thoughts and memories. Suddenly, she broke her silence, saying, "I won't be back, will I?"

Before I could think of how to answer that question, she pleaded, "But you will, won't you? Promise me you will! Promise me!"

"I promise, Sony! I promise," I repeated, but she was already staring that distant look way down the road to nowhere.

SONY REMEMBERS

By the time we got back to Pennsylvania, I wanted to sleep for a week, but I needed to prepare a presentation for a large group of educators in western New York, so deep sleep was delayed.

Sony continued her decline. She was sleeping more and eating less. Even ice cream didn't interest her. When she was awake, her thoughts were scrambled and words difficult to follow. This became her new norm. Sony no longer recognized me, or the stories I'd tell her.

The day before I left for my speaking engagement, I stopped in to see Sony and was shocked to see her sitting up in bed and totally alert. I had been there the day before to feed her, and she didn't say a word. In fact, she kept forgetting how to swallow.

"David!" she shouted as I entered her room. "I was just thinking about you. Do you remember the time when you and Terry and I were in Rome, and we went to that concert in the ruins?

"Terry and I got all dressed up in those fancy dresses we'd bought in Paris and had stuffed them in our backpacks, hoping we'd find an occasion to wear them. It was a gorgeous night, and the three of us took a carriage ride to the concert. Remember Mama? The woman who owned the little pension where we were staying. She lent me a scarf because she thought my dress showed too much cleavage. Sit here on my bed," Sony insisted, and I did. She went on and on about things we'd done and places we'd visited.

I was shocked! I had not seen this side of Sony in years and was torn between running to get a nurse to witness this event and staying so I wouldn't miss a second of the conversation.

She talked in great detail about our trip to Budapest and visiting Terry's non-English-speaking relatives in the rolling landscape of the Hungarian farmland.

A moment later, she was recalling a hillside on the edge of Luxemburg where Terry, Sony, and I had spread out our sleeping bags in the dark and slept the night. In the morning, we discovered that we were camping on one of the city's main walking paths. Workers were stepping over and around us, trying not to disturb our sleep as our wind-up alarm clock ticked away on Sony's pillow.

"What do you remember about Egypt?" I asked, eager to hear the depths of her memory.

"Everything," she laughed. "We rode camels to the pyramids! Then there was that terrible accident we witnessed when a young dark-skinned man tried to climb over the spiked iron fence to see the Sphinx. He fell and hung there in the paralyzing heat, impaled and dying."

"I remember thinking how many people travel thousands of miles to see the mummy of a dead pharaoh, and no one ran to help this man."

"You tried, David, remember? You ran to get a guard and were told they'd get to it when they get to it."

"I remember the guard saying, 'There are almost ten million people in Cairo! One less doesn't matter.'"

"He was still hanging there, dead, when our driver pulled away."

"Human life doesn't have the same value in different places around the world. A lot can depend on the color of your skin, slant of your eyes, or way you express your beliefs.

"Sony, do you remember the old Egyptian we met who was making sand art in the desert?"

"Yes. He was amazing, sitting there cross-legged, all dressed in loose white cotton contrasted against the sameness of the beige Sahara. He'd scoop up a handful of ordinary sand and cast it across a square piece of wood that was cradled in his lap. Then he'd begin tapping individual grains of sand with a glass rod, chasing them into different piles. Soon, it became apparent that he was organizing them according to color.

"Looking out at the vast desert, it all seemed the same, but he was able to detect differences by using the tip of the glass rod as a magnifier. From these piles of deep red, blue, and every other color across the spectrum, he filled small glass bottles with an array of colors in layers as a reminder that we have to look carefully to see and appreciate the beauty of diversity."

An hour passed, and I still did not move off Sony's bed, then she looked back at me as if she were still in Egypt and said, "The sun is too bright," and closed her eyes. They never opened again.

Mary called me with the news of Sony's death. She said it was peaceful and without pain. I called Gordon, emphasizing the peaceful pain-free part of her departure and saying I'd be out to visit him soon.

HOSPITAL NUMBER 3

Gordon's transfer to the Veteran's Hospital came without much warning. I was up on a ladder at his house, repairing a long crack in the ceiling of his living room when the phone rang. The crack had opened up following one of the many tremors that frequently rattled the area. I wanted it patched and painted in case he was released from the hospital. I figured evidence of earthquake activity would be the last thing Gordon would want to see.

I showered, dressed, and drove to his current healthcare facility, just in time to follow the ambulance from his second hospital to his third and desired Veteran's Hospital.

As always, the traffic was horrendous, but this time, I stuck right behind the ambulance whose siren was blaring, reminding drivers just who had the right of way. I was also able to access the hospital through the employee's entrance. This eliminated the strain of trying to find a parking space and walking in the heat to the front of the building, crowded with long-term patients, seeking to catch a glimpse of blue skies.

Again, there was a pile of papers to negotiate and new doctors to meet, each wanting to know my connection to the patient. By the time I got to see Gordon in his new room, he was already charming one of the nurses with his humor.

"Watch out for this one," I said as I entered his room. "He loves a pretty face."

"You must be his brother," she responded. "Does chasing skirts run in the family?"

"Never mind him. He's an old married man!" Gordon piped up as she exited with a smile. "I'm finally here! I made it! The bed is right, and the nurse is pretty."

"And what's our next step?" I questioned.

"Healing! But that's something I have to do. You got me here, and now you have to go home to your family."

"What's this? I'm being dismissed? My job is done?"

"You have a different assignment! I didn't want to mention this, but since you're pressing the issue, I'll give it to you straight. I've listened patiently to you every time you've visited, and you need some new material! I've heard all your stories and—"

"And what? You're bored?"

"You've got to hit the road. Get on a plane, climb a mountain, have an adventure! Your job is to scout out some new stories and share them when the doctors say I'm ready to go home."

"Are you sure you don't want me to hang around for a while?"

"And do what? Sit by my bed and tell me shit I've already heard? You've been gone from home for quite a while already, and I love you for it! If you stay, you'll only ruin my chances with that nurse. You have no idea how hard it is for a quad to compete for a pretty girl's attention."

"When should I leave?"

"Soon! Leave tomorrow morning and get right to work. Travel someplace different this time. Fill my head with things I've never imagined."

"You'll miss me when I'm gone."

"I miss you already!"

"I'll leave tomorrow under one condition."

"What? You want that nurse tonight?"

"I want you to heal! I want to get that call from the doctor, saying you're ready to be released. I'll fly out and bring you home. I promise to get some new material for exciting stories, if you do that for me."

"It's a deal," he said. "Now get the hell out of here! By the way, if you see that nurse, tell her my pillow needs fluffing. That's code in hospital talk," he said with a wink.

I laughed and then left to go back to his place and pack.

Early the next morning, I met Steve at Starbucks. All the usual characters were there, and now I was one of them. Steve said he'd check in on Gordon regularly and call if there were any concerns.

I liked and trusted him. I knew he would be there for Gordon, and most importantly, I knew that Steve was a true friend!

The trip back to Pennsylvania was relatively uneventful. I stopped to hike in a couple of national parks and visited an elderly aunt in Indiana, but for the most part, I just drove.

The journey had taken more out of me than I had realized, and home was all I could think about. I wanted to get there as badly as Gordon wanted to get to his home.

I didn't come across any outrageous and memorable characters or experiences that would have piqued Gordon's interest. Unlike the trip west, my thoughts were not linked to the past and years of shared stories. All those memories seemed like a book I'd been reading and loved but lost before I could read the last few pages.

I talked to Terry every night to share my thoughts as well as my cross-country progress. I wanted to sleep in my own bed, put my arms around her, and thank her for all the years we'd shared together.

Terry had seen me when I was on top of the world and when the world was on top of me! Through it all, she understood my need to be held close and to be set free. She never saw these needs as contradictory but rather that which made me whole.

She also accepted without question the people that I brought into our world, like Sony and Gordon and Wilma and Mary and hundreds of others who helped flesh out the different parts of me that needed to be revealed.

Terry embraced and enhanced our life of home, traditions, children, grandchildren, and friends as we pursued continuous education, theater, arts, and adventure. All this and more made me want to hold her.

When I finally turned into our driveway, I wanted to cry and didn't even know why.

OUT OF PRISON

Three months later, I received a call from Gordon.

"I'm getting out of prison! Can you pick me up? I'll be released in two days! I can't wait to get home! I need to be in my own bed, see my drawings, and drink a fucking beer! I can arrange for an ambulance ride, if you can't make it."

"I'll make it," I answered. "I'll get a reservation as soon as we hang up. I don't want your homecoming to include an ambulance! We're putting all that behind us.

"You start making plans for what we'll do during my visit, and they better include some time at Laguna Beach, a movie, and some tacos!"

"Will you be able to stay for a while?"

"Not too long. I have an art show coming up, and Terry and I have made plans to go hiking in Europe."

I got a reservation for a flight that would put me in LA the day before his release. I figured I'd visit Gordon immediately and then go to his house to make sure everything was in order. I also had to make arrangements for all his health services to begin.

I rented a car and drove directly to the hospital, parking right in front near the main entrance where all the quads gathered.

From the moment I exited my car, all eyes were on me. Heads turned, tilting forward, eyes focused without blinking at the stranger in their midst.

Their stares made me self-conscious. I felt increasingly clumsy with every step. I awkwardly tried to find my stride while sweating across the parking lot, concentrating on the sign at the front of the hospital that read, "Spinal Care Unit."

The closer I got to the door, the more eyes investigated my every move, shamelessly looking for a limp, a paralyzed arm, crippled hand, bandages, scars, crutches, cane, walker, anything hinting that I was part of the club.

The sidewalk was crowded with the permanently seated, lifted from their beds and assisted to the out of doors for fresh air and blue skies. There, they are parked to glimpse a world that goes on without them.

Each silent sun catcher followed my every step. I heard unspoken words and responded in kind, save the occasional hello murmured before they close their eyes and roll back into the shade.

I wanted them to know! I wanted them to accept me as a temporary member of their society. I wanted to tell them that a stroke had taken away my ability to speak, to walk, or use the right side of my body. It twisted my face and scrambled my brain. But I recovered! I walk and am not eligible to be anything more than a guest in a world where recovery is the stuff of dreams.

Through the door and across the foyer toward the elevator, I maneuvered the maze of wheels and feet that never touch the floor, keeping my eyes from meeting other eyes.

Spotting stairs that led to the second floor, I bolted up two at a time. I was unaware until I reached the turn at the landing that jealous eyes had followed me with dreams of football games and dancing.

I had been at the Veteran's Hospital many times, but every time feels like the first time. I never get used to it, or the feeling that perhaps one of those men in their wheelchair is someone I was in the Army with, someone not so lucky.

Many of them still wear their US military fatigue hat with pins signifying certain campaigns or rank.

I'd walked though those front doors multiple times over the last forty years, and it never gets easier. I had been here three months earlier to visit Gordon, and some of the same men were sitting in the same spots, waiting. They wait for family or friends or death. Sometimes the family and friends don't come, but death always does.

His eyes washed over me like spring rain the instant he looked up from his bed. He called my name, and I went to his side. He looked frail and tried to hide behind an enthusiastic greeting.

"You came!" he repeated several times, each time more like a whisper than the time before.

"Of course, I came," I responded. "We've got to get you home!"

Home was the only thing he dared to want anymore.

He was weak and thin, and I realized immediately the real reason why he was going home, and that once I got him there, he wouldn't be going out again!

I strapped him into the van to go for a ride. We drove down to Laguna Beach and then through the winding steep and narrow streets that led up to the top of the high and sandy cliffs. This was where Gordon asked to get out of the van to get a better view of the vast blue Pacific.

We'd come to this particular vantage point many times before, but this time, he wanted to maneuver his wheelchair closer to the edge. He rolled ten feet, stopped, and then rolled another three before rolling another two without ever taking his eyes off the horizon. I hurried anxiously to stay by his side.

"I think that's close enough," I warned, but he kept rolling until his wheels were inches from the cliff's edge before stopping.

I stood there, poised, and ready, placing my hand firmly on his shoulder.

The stiff ocean breeze pushed his hair this way and that way as he squinted into the sun, trying to get a glimpse of Catalina Island in the distance.

"This reminds me of that story you once told me of when you went paragliding off that cliff in Switzerland. Was the mountain breeze anything like this?"

"Just like this, Gordon, only colder! It was a remarkable experience. The expert tandem pilot spread out the nylon wings, strapped me into the harness, adjusted my helmet, and then tied himself in. He told me to stand up straight along with him and wait until he counted to three. On three, we were to run together off the cliff and keep running until I could feel the wind pulling the support up underneath me. Then I was to hold on and enjoy the ride."

"What did it feel like?"

"Completely liberating! It was total freedom. It was as if I was the wind itself! We caught an updraft and soared thousands of feet into the sky. We even did a complete loop. There I was—upside down in space—and I didn't even lose my lunch!"

"What was your favorite part?"

"There were two. I absolutely loved running off the cliff! I had made a decision, committed to it, and followed through."

"And the second?"

"The pilot asked me if I wanted to handle the controls and determine my own direction."

"Did you?"

"You bet I did!"

Gordon and I lingered a long time in silence on the edge of that cliff before backing up and returning to the van.

He was quiet as we drove to our favorite bar where I got him out of the van, found a place where we could sit outside in the sun, eat Mexican food, drink a beer, and talk.

We didn't even pretend that tomorrow we'd go someplace, do something special, and have an adventure.

He looked, not at me but into me and asked where Terry and I were planning to hike. I gave him the overview, emphasizing the parts I knew he'd like best. I talked of street life in Florence, filled with interesting shops with open fronts packed with cheeses of every sort, hanging aged salami and bowls of fresh herbs, filling the air with the scent of rosemary, parsley, oregano, basil, and sage. I painted him a picture of the cathedral and bell tower, the Italian food, museums, the beautiful women, and the mountain views!

"I'll go with you," he said with a wink. "I have my passport," he smiled.

He did not expect a reply, and I did not give one.

I reached across the table to clink the lip of his beer glass with mine.

"Wear my shoes when you go, David! Climb a mountain with me! Take Terry dancing! Give those shoes a workout."

"I will, Gordon! I will. What kind of dance would you like?"

"Nothing fancy! No twirls or crazy steps. A waltz would be nice. Hold her close!"

The next ten days were a whirlwind of urine bags, medical musts, paperwork, spasms, medications, conversations, and sleep. There were good days and setbacks and then it was time for me to go.

We just looked at each other. No words were needed. We'd spent forty years connected by words that made up the stories we shared. Now words were hard to find.

"I'll be back, Gordon!"

"I won't be here, David! You've been my tandem pilot for decades, but now it's time for me to solo!"

"Are you afraid?"

"Not anymore. Existing is not living! It took me a long time to take over the controls. In order to live, you can't be afraid to die! I'm no longer afraid to do either."

I folded my fingers and bumped his frozen fist—just two guys saying goodbye!

Back in Pennsylvania, Terry and I completed our plans for a trip to visit friends who live in the Black Forest region of Germany. We left on August 20, 2018. I wore Gordon's shoes!

After Germany, we went hiking in the Dolomites, staying at Hotel Pider in the La Valle / Wengen region. Our days were filled with photographing the spectacular mountain range and finding just the right spot to sit with our watercolors and paint.

On September 1, we left for Florence, Italy, where we rented our favorite apartment.

Terry took classes in Italian and art history, and I investigated every corner of that famous city.

I hiked and wrote and painted during the day and then made supper, which we ate while sitting on our balcony, sharing our day's experiences along with a bottle of red wine.

Then it was off to the opera or a lecture or out for gelato near the Ponte Santa Trinita, one of the many bridges that spans the Arno River.

This particular bridge offered the best view of the iconic medieval Ponte Vecchio in one direction and the sunset in the other.

This is where we danced, turning slowly in the evening breeze, catching a glimpse of the ancient structure bathed in gold upstream and the fabulous orange, red, purples, and pinks of the setting sun downstream.

We didn't need music. It was in us. We held each other and moved slow and easy, like the waters flowing under the bridge.

Life was simple, filled with conversation, pasta salads, red wine, and laughter.

My thoughts were in the moment, saturated with the now that I love so much.

After leaving Florence, we went to hike along the coastal mountains of Cinqua Terra. Then on October 2, we took a train to Frankfurt. This would be our last evening in Europe before flying home the next day.

As we were packing, the phone rang. It was Robert, the aide I'd hired for Gordon.

He said that Gordon died peacefully at home in his own bed surrounded by all the postcards and letters we had sent during our trip.

My brother died holding his passport in his hands!

Epilogue

Terry and I flew to California to organize a *celebration-of-life party* in Gordon's home. Along with Steve, health-care workers, and neighbors, there were freshly cut flowers, stories, and laughter shared with food and wine and beer.

All of Gordon's portraits were on display as silent witnesses to his life.

I sent Gordon's special nurse the check as he had requested!

I also called her, and we cried together for all that had been and all that might have been.

Afterward, we emptied Gordon's house, and donated pots and pans, dishes, bowls, silverware, books, beds, blankets, and furniture.

We gave away medical equipment, vans, and wheelchairs and packed what we wanted in a rented truck.

Finally, we cleaned the place, and sold it!

We paid off his medical expenses, other bills, and closed all accounts.

Terry and I drove the truck containing the wood carving of a cat, Gordon's collection of prints, and all his fabulous drawings back to Pennsylvania along with Gordon's ashes.

*****

I always saw my brother as a rolling miracle. And me, I am the one who periodically had the privilege of being his legs. I brought my brother stories gathered from all corners of the world alive with color and noise and movement. My brother brought me the courage to be still. In that stillness, I wrote this book.

ABOUT THE AUTHOR

D. C. Page has often been called a Renaissance man. His life is filled with artistic expression and productivity. He writes, paints, performs, and encourages others to reach their full potential. Trained in the arts, education, administration, and leadership, David has traveled all over the country, sharing his love of creative efforts. In his free time, David can be found hiking with his wife in the Swiss Alps, Italian Dolomites, or anywhere there is an adventure to be had or beautiful scene to paint.